Swimming
with the
Sharks

For Eric, who supports me in every way
and fills my life with laughter.

Acknowledgments

My sincerest thanks to my insightful editor Andrew Karre, who inspired me to dig deep, and to all the good people at Flux; my agent Steven Chudney, for making my dream a reality; Joyce Sweeney, friend and mentor; Norma Davids, Dorian Cirrone, Alex Flinn, Adrienne Sylver, Danielle Joseph, Linda Rodriguez-Bernfeld, Kathy MacDonald, Gloria Rothstein, and Melody Samuelson; teen experts Jennifer Moss, Sarah Otto, and Stacey Marineau; Mark Chaykin of the US Cheerleading Association; Sherry Grossman for generously proofing my cheerleading scenes; my family and friends for their support: Sara and Donald Reed, Danny and Joyce Reed, David Reed, Anita and Donald Fischer, Karen and Paul Margolies, Jenifer and Marc Lewison, Randi Frazin, Bonnie Reiver, Keri Leibowitz, Debbie Zebersky, Lauri Sokoloff, Stacey Zedeck, Marianne Altschul, Laura Sherry, Lisa Siemens, Cheryl Bloom, Nikki Weisburd, and Karen Barr; and my treasures, Eric, Louis, and Sam.

Swimming
with the
Sharks

Debbie Reed Fischer

Woodbury, Minnesota

First Edition
First Printing, 2008

Book design by Steffani Sawyer
Cover design by Kevin R. Brown
Female cheerleader jumping in air: ©2008 Victoria Snowber/
   Digital Vision/Punchstock
Cheerleaders talking on cell phones: ©2008 Jupiter Images/Brand X
   Pictures/Punchstock

Flux, an imprint of Llewellyn Publications

Library of Congress Cataloging-in-Publication Data

Fischer, Debbie Reed, 1967–
  Swimming with the sharks / Debbie Reed Fischer.—1st ed.
    p. cm.
  ISBN 978-0-7387-1161-4
  1. Teenage girls—Fiction. 2. Schools—Fiction. 3. High
schools—Fiction. 4. Dating (Social customs)—Fiction. 5.
Interpersonal relations—Fiction. I. Title.
  PS3606.I765S95 2008
  813'.6—dc22

                            2008012990

Flux
Llewellyn Publications
A Division of Llewellyn Worldwide, Ltd.
2143 Wooddale Drive, Dept. 978-0-7387-1161-4
Woodbury, MN 55125-2989, U.S.A.
www.fluxnow.com

Printed in the United States of America

The list is titled *Top Ten Guys Who Are Still Virgins*. Dorkowitz tops it off at number one, of course. His real name is David Dornowitz, but no one's called him David since third grade. When our coach, Miss Wisser, found the list tacked up on our *News to Cheer About* bulletin board, I knew we'd get detention. And we did, the whole varsity cheerleading squad. So now I have to stay after school and it's only the first day of the year.

But I really don't mind all that much, to be honest. In fact, I'm secretly excited to be included in the punishment. It means I'm officially in. No more standing on the social sidelines for me. Now that I'm on varsity, I'll finally be an Alpha.

It sounds pathetic, I know, but this detention should seal the deal. And I'm ready. Because, to be even more honest, if that virgin list were for girls, number one would be me: Peyton Grady, president of the Neverhadaboyfriend Club.

Nobody would tell Coach Wisser who wrote the list, even though we all knew it was Lexie Court, our captain. So instead of just Lexie getting in trouble, we all did. Maya Kaplan, my best friend since kindergarten, says that I'm the perfect example of America's insecure youth being manipulated by the shallow masses. She also says cheering is for ding-dongs, and asks why I waste my brain power jumping around.

Maya's waiting for me outside the cafetorium for the annual welcome assembly. She's tapping her watch. I'm late, as usual. "Peyton, you have a serious lateness issue."

"I prefer to be called punctually challenged." I flick an eyelash off of Maya's cheek.

"Punctually challenged. I'll have to remember that one for my shrink." We roll our eyes at each other. Maya's parents just made her start seeing a psychologist. They told her, after reading the latest parenting bestseller, that they're concerned she may have identity issues due to being both biracial and Jewish.

We both think it's a crock. What are identity issues anyway? What problems do they think she has? Maya's the most well-grounded person I know.

There's nothing wrong with Maya, which is exactly what's wrong with Maya. Unlike me—five foot eleven, freckled, and flat as a surfboard—she's petite and perfect. I feel like a giraffe when I stand next to her. Maya's like a character straight out of a Hollywood teen movie: pretty, brilliant, president of a million extracurricular clubs, your basic perfectionista. And if that's not enough, her most amazing trait is that she's welcomed by every single clique at Beachwood, from the drama geeks to the Alphas. I wish I knew her secret.

"These assemblies are such a waste," I say, pushing the heavy door open for both of us. "I mean, aren't they always telling us to use our time constructively?"

"Totally," Maya agrees. "I'd rather be in class." The cafetorium lights are off and some movie about fire safety is on the screen, which no one's bothering to watch. The lunch tables are stacked against the walls and chairs are lined up in rows. Our auditorium would be so much better for assemblies, but Dr. Giles, the drama teacher, insists that the thea-tah be reserved for her sacred plays.

Maya and I scan the room for good seats. I spot my squad and some guys on the football team taking up one of the middle rows. The guys are all wearing their letter jackets even though it's ninety degrees out. Lexie and her best friend Beth Ann, a Scarlett Johansson look-alike, wave at us to come sit with them. I check Maya's face for approval. "Want to sit over there?" I'm dying to sit with them. I want the whole school to see my new status.

"Sure. Sloane's cool." Sloane is on the squad and she also writes for our school paper, *The Beachwood Beacon*, with Maya and me. Maya's the editor in chief. I decide we should sit in the row just behind them. After all, they're seniors and we're still juniors. The JV cheerleaders are sitting in the back with the other freshman and sophomores.

At Beachwood Preparatory Academy, most people are measured, boxed, and labeled clearly. You have to be careful where you sit, who you say hi to, even who you make eye contact with. These are all major decisions that can affect your whole social life. Of course, it's positively magical how none of the above ever affects Maya.

The senior cheerleaders are lounging back in their seats with their feet on the chairs in front of them. Lexie's silky layers of baby-blonde hair hang perfectly down her back. From where I sit, her profile is perfection. Her nose is just the right size for her face, her full lips pucker all by themselves, and her dark, almond-shaped eyes have the longest lashes I've ever seen.

"Hey, look," she calls out, "it's number one." She points her manicured finger to the aisle, where Dorkowitz is headed. The thing about Dorkowitz is that, well, he's exactly what you're picturing. A chinless, cowlick-bobbing, pants-too-short, glasses-aimed-at-the-floor, hands-jammed-in-his-pockets nerd. It's like someone called a casting director and said, "What we need is the nerdiest-looking nerd on the planet." Right now he's headed toward the bathrooms. He's walking really fast, probably to get past the Alphas as quickly as possible. I wonder if he's heard about the list.

"Looks like number one has to make number one," says Hunter, Lexie's boyfriend.

Beth Ann's boyfriend, Justin, calls out, "Yo, Dorkowitz! Dude, you're number one! How does it feel?" To make matters worse for poor Dorkowitz, the soles of his sneakers are making these loud, farting noises every time he takes a step on the varnished wood floor.

"Naw, sounds like number one has to make a number two," yells a freshman sitting a few rows back, and some people start cracking up. Then the freshman decides to add some sound effects with the old armpit-and-hand trick. Everyone's laughing now. The teachers shush us, on autopilot. As I pointed out, no one's watching the movie.

I smile along with the others and try not to think about how Dorkowitz was my lab partner last year. I have to admit he was a pretty good lab partner. He always offered to dissect the gross parts I didn't want to touch, and he always gave me all his notes. He even shared a few of his test answers with me from time to time when the need arose.

The movie's over, and we all settle down a little. Lights come on and Dr. Johnson, our headmaster, drones on and on about school safety. I see Sloane writing in her notebook. It's probably a poem for Diego, her trophy boyfriend at U of Miami.

Sloane's been trying forever to get Maya to print her puke-provoking love poetry in the *Beacon*, but Maya keeps telling her to stick to writing "Shark Bites," her gossip column. I write "Last Look," on the back page, which covers student highlights. My first story this year will be about our pep rally and the start of football season this Friday.

I decide to use my time constructively and get some homework done. For AP English we're supposed to write a review of our summer reading, *Lord of the Flies.* I already did that last period, in math. We're also supposed to write a detailed description of someone, using evocative language and sensory details. I take out a sheet of paper and write:

> *Dr. Johnson is wearing a vintage polyester sky-blue suit, a fat tie circa 1976, and matching sky-blue Hush Puppies. He is not wearing this to be retro-cool, like some of my irony-loving class-mates who wear Keep on Truckin' T-shirts and call everything "radical," but because he bought them when they were in style and he hasn't bought new clothes since. His bald spot is cleverly hidden with a sweep of greased hair starting from a part above his left ear and ending above his right ear. His skin is white and pasty, evoking visions of the powdered mashed potatoes and feet loaf we had today for lunch.*

Maya interrupts my writing. "There's your BOM."

"Where?" My eyes dart around, searching. "And he's not my BOM." Maya calls every guy I like my Boy o' the Month, or BOM for short. It's true that I usually don't stay interested in a guy for that long, but Von Cohen is differ-ent. I've had a major crush on him since last year. "Is he looking at me?"

"No. And it's too bad, 'cause you look hot today, girlfriend." I actually do look pretty good because I'm wearing the pleated navy skirt our dress code requires for Mondays, and mine is a lot shorter than it's supposed to be. The Beachwood handbook states that "the length of girls' skirts must be no more than three inches above the knees." Ha. As if. One of the few advantages of being a human totem pole is having long legs, so I make the most of mine by folding over the waistband of my skirt, shortening it into a mid-thigh mini. A lot of girls do it, and the teachers never say anything.

"Where is he?" I ask, frantically smoothing down my flat-ironed hair.

"Front row. With all his skater buddies," she says. I spot him. His sandy-blond hair is hanging over his eyes, and he's flicking it off his face. He's playing a game on his Sidekick. There's a band-aid over his earlobe, hiding an earring so he won't get reported for being out of uniform.

Omigod. He's unbuttoning his collar, loosening his tie. He is so extremely hot. He needs to shave, and I try to imagine what his stubbly chin feels like, what he smells like. My face flushes.

All the kids are clapping. I peel my eyes away from Von. Fifteen students are standing behind Dr. Johnson on the stage. "Thank you for giving your new classmates a warm welcome into the Beachwood family," he says with zero enthusiasm. "And now, let's get to know them." Every year he parades the new kids out with a big speech about how it's a major deal to get accepted into Beachwood, since it's the most selective private school in Florida and aren't we all lucky.

I'm lucky I got accepted in kindergarten because I would die of embarrassment if I had to tower over everyone on stage like King Kong on display for the crowds. Dr. Johnson introduces each new student in his trademark monotone. It sounds like he's underwater.

One new student is really strange. She's a squatty stump of a girl, barrel-shaped, wearing thick, orange eyeglasses. She's smiling wildly at us cheerleaders like we should all know her. Her mousey hair is in a sideways ponytail. Seriously. A sideways ponytail. Isn't that the international symbol of girl geekdom?

"Who is *that?*" Beth Ann asks Lexie.

"More like *what* is that?" she answers.

"And now I'd like to present Ellika Garret," Dr. Johnson announces, and the girl steps forward. At the mention of her name, a lot of kids whisper and snicker. Everyone's heard of the Garrets.

"Garret?" Maya groans. "As in the Garrets who donated the fundage to build the GAF?"

"Has to be," I answer. The Garret Athletic Facility, a.k.a. the GAF, is our new gym. It's amazing, with two gymnasiums, carpeted locker rooms, a state-of-the-art weight room with mirrored walls, the works. "It's a good thing she has all that money, because she doesn't have anything else going for her."

"That's for sure," Maya agrees.

"Just look at that chunky monkey," says Devin, the loudest one on our squad. "And what's with the Larry King glasses?"

"They're too queer," Lexie agrees. "Hasn't she heard of contacts? And hello, what about the hair? She needs a makeover."

"I know you'll all make Ellika feel at home here at Beachwood," drones Dr. Johnson lifelessly. The obnoxious freshman in the back starts fake coughing the words "Ellika Smellika" into his hand. A chorus of "Smellika" coughs echo around the cafetorium.

Dr. Johnson ignores the coughers and pushes on, his voice sagging with every word. "That her surname is emblazoned on our athletic center is quite apropos, since Ellika will also be gracing our varsity cheerleading squad."

"What?" Lexie squeaks, sitting up.

"Did he just say what I think he said?" Beth Ann asks. Dr. Johnson sweeps his arm toward the stubby girl like he's unveiling a brand new car on *The Price is Right*. She waves maniacally toward us and bounces. Ellika Garret looks about as athletic as one of those TV geriatrics who exercise sitting in a chair.

"Oh. My. God," Lexie practically shouts. The whole squad starts talking all at once.

"It's got to be a mistake. He's not serious."

"She wasn't even at tryouts."

"Look at her. She's a blob."

"No way. We've never even seen this loser before and suddenly she's on the squad? I don't think so."

I just keep saying, "Where's Coach Wisser? We have to get her," but no one's listening. Coach Wisser, our sponsor and everyone's favorite teacher, will fix this. She just graduated college two years ago and she's young and cool and will totally take our side. She has to. There's no way this weird girl is going to slide into a spot on our squad. Not without a fight. And I know Coach Wisser will fight for us.

"She doesn't look like a cheerleader," says Maya.

"She's not. She can't be," I answer.

I'm lucky I made it onto varsity. I'm one of only a handful of JV who made it this year. Coach Wisser says my height isn't any problem because I'm a good dancer, plus I'm strong and the squad needs me as a base for lifts.

For two years, I paid my dues putting up with all the JV hazing. My hair's never been the same since last year's varsity squad put honey in our shampoo at winter cheer camp. And I worked my butt off practice after practice, game after game. So I'm just as mad as everybody else about someone thinking they can get on the squad without working for it. "We need Coach Wisser," I say again.

Teachers shush us, wanting us to be quiet and stop being so disrespectful. Lexie whispers, "Peyton's right. We need Wisser." Lexie doesn't give out credit very often. I'm so warm and fuzzy I'm probably glowing, like ET's heart. "Let's meet in Wisser's office after detention. She always stays late."

"I bet that girl can't even do the splits," Maya says after school. We're walking to her BMW 325. Yup, she really has a BMW. And it's not the only one in the student parking lot. "How's she going to do cheers?"

"She won't be doing any." I'm scoping the crowds for Von so I can accidentally-on-purpose wind up next to him. Kids are still pouring out of the main building. "She'll never be allowed on the squad. Lexie'll never let it happen."

"Don't be so sure. Her parents donated the GAF. Johnson will give her whatever she wants. Hey, he better not give her a student council spot." Maya is vice president this year. She's already planning her spring campaign for the presidency. "Is your mom working tonight?"

"Yeah."

"Want to come over for dinner?" She looks hopeful.

"I can't. Remember, I have detention," I say with pride.

"You better not get too many of those, you know." She uses her prissy voice. "Two more's a suspension and then you could lose your scholarship, and how would that look on a college application?"

I stop walking and glare at her, surprised. Maya never brings that up. No one does. It's okay if I bring up my scholarship, which I never do, but it's not okay if anyone else does, even Maya. I can feel my mouth pinching into a straight line.

"I'm sorry, I didn't mean it that way." She sounds nervous. I can't answer her. She's out of line. And besides, I'm not done glaring. "I'm sorry, Peyton. I just, you know, I always think that way."

"What way?" I fold my arms.

"I don't know," she says, flustered. "I'm always thinking about the future, lately."

"What does that have to do with my ..." I hesitate. I almost say "scholarship," but decide on, "situation?"

Maya shrugs. "It's just that you're so into this cheerleading thing." She says the word "cheerleading" like it tastes bad. "This is an important year, you know. There's SATs, GPAs, recommendations. What if you—"

"Don't worry about me." Lately, she's been in worrying mode more often. Sometimes Maya thinks it's her job to worry about me or something. "I have no intention of getting suspended, or losing ... anything." What does she know about financial worries? Her dad is the top plastic surgeon in Boca Raton.

Maya holds up her hands in surrender. "Okay, okay, I'm sorry. Forget I said anything." We walk for a little bit, not talking. Kids are everywhere, chatting, laughing, and getting in their cars. I hear a radio playing rap music. Maya links her arm with mine. "Don't be mad, Pey. Come for dinner. After detention, I mean."

"Is Magda baking brownies?" I ask. I'm such a sucker. Maya irritates me sometimes, but I can never stay mad at her.

"I doubt it. She's pissed at my mother this week. She says Mom spoke to her like a maid."

"But she is a maid."

"That's beside the point."

"So there's no brownies?"

"Probably not. But come anyway."

We're at Maya's car. "You know I'd love to, but we've also got this emergency meeting. I think it'll get too late."

She climbs in and shuts the door. "I guess I'll catch you *mañana.*"

"*Mañana*, it is. We're still on for Friday, right?" I usually sleep over on Fridays, although I haven't in a long time because Maya was on a teen tour of Europe all summer. Then, when she came back, I went away to cheer camp with the squad.

"Definitely."

"Call me tonight," I say as she backs out.

"I will," she shouts out her window, driving away. "I want to hear all the juicy details about the meeting."

Who is she kidding? Maya could care less about a cheer meeting. But I play along and shout back, "I'll tell you everything!"

2

Everyone takes Mrs. Pavlich's astronomy elective because it's a total joke. Mrs. Pavlich is about a hundred and five years old and has absolutely no control over the class. Plus she doesn't make us take notes, doesn't give any homework, and best of all, the whole school knows that her study guides make up the actual test. She just puts the questions in a different order.

Her class is the perfect relaxation before my seventh period trigonometry nightmare, a class I'm in grave danger of failing unless some Higher Power suddenly flips on the lights in the math room of my brain. Right now, it's pitch black in there.

Astronomy, on the flip side, is a party. A lot of Alphas and troublemakers are in this class, and it's the high point of my day. I sit in the back where all the fun is. Today

Hunter and Justin have a bet to see how many times they can make Mrs. Pavlich say Uranus. Lexie's keeping score.

"The rings around Uranus can't be seen with the naked eye," warbles Mrs. Pavlich.

"How do you know?" Justin calls out. "Have you looked at Uranus?"

"Oh, yes. I've looked at it many times." Our shoulders shake with giggles.

"You've looked at what many times?" asks Hunter.

"Uranus, dear. Pay attention."

"Nine to seven," Lexie says. "Justin's winning."

"I'd pay attention if you were looking at Uranus," says Justin. "Although I don't think I'd want to see something like that." We all explode. Even Kim Wu, the most serious girl I know, can't help smiling a little and sneaking peeks over her shoulder from the front row. The only one who's tuned out (besides Mrs. Pavlich, of course) is Sloane, who's flipping through *InStyle* magazine.

"What's so funny?" asks Mrs. Pavlich pleasantly. She chuckles a little, making her neck flab wobble.

"Yeah, what's so funny?" Dorkowitz asks no one in particular, pushing his glasses up. No one answers him or Mrs. Pavlich, so he goes back to doodling, which is what he's always doing in this class. Not even Dorkowitz bothers to take notes on Planet Pavlich. He's doing a pretty good sketch of a ninja.

"Exactly how do you look at Uranus, Mrs. Pavlich?" Hunter asks, cupping his chin in his hand as if he's serious.

"Well, with a telescope, of course."

"You looked at Uranus with a telescope?" Hunter yells.

"Oh, yes indeed," says Mrs. Pavlich, puzzled by the hilarity.

"Ouch. That's gotta hurt." I'm laughing so hard that my sides ache. Lexie, Beth Ann, and I are all doubled over, watching each other crack up.

Ellika Garret is sitting one row in front of us, laughing the loudest in this really forced, fake way and trying to make eye contact, but we all ignore her. At the beginning of class she called out, "Hey, guys," and tried to hand out gum to us, but nobody accepted. We're under strict instructions not to look at or speak to her unless necessary, and when we do we're supposed to call her Smellika. Our first practice with her, tomorrow, should be interesting. Only Lexie has had direct contact with her so far.

Lexie's given a lot of instructions about how to handle Smellika since our meeting with Coach Wisser a few days ago. The meeting didn't go so well. Lexie shouted that it wasn't fair, that as captain she should be consulted, that letting in "someone like her" isn't what we've worked for, that she'll bring the squad down and ruin our reputation.

Coach Wisser kept twisting her long, brown hair, avoiding our eyes. She claimed her hands were tied because the board feels strongly that Ellika Garret will be an asset to our varsity squad. What crap. It's so obvious that the Garrets just want payback. I couldn't believe she said it with a straight face.

Coach Wisser also said Ellika left Palm Glades Prep because she was having trouble fitting in. *"Quelle surprise,"* said Lexie. Then Coach Wisser had the nerve to tell us we should all try to make her feel like part of the squad. "Part of the squad, my ass," was Lexie's response, followed by "no effing way." In the end, we tried every argument we could think of and even made our moms call to complain, but we're still stuck with her.

Lexie held her own meeting after the meeting, without Coach Wisser. She told us not to worry, because although Smellika may technically be on varsity with us, she'll still have to go through the same "initiation rituals" as a JV girl. And not just routine hazing, like wearing your clothes backwards or being someone's personal slave for a week.

Lexie wants to go hard core. Her plan is to make Ellika Garret suffer, make her life so miserable that she'll want to leave. "The only way to get her off the squad for good is to drive her fat ass out of Beachwood," she said. "So, here's the sitch. We're going to take the initiation rituals to the next level, break her down bit by bit until there's no way she'll want to stay." The goal is to have her gone by next semester.

Lexie is a born motivational speaker. She really pumped us up, saying, "We can do it, all of us, together. I'm counting on each and every one of you. You've worked hard to be the best. So screw the board, and screw Smellika. We're taking our squad back."

Lexie's plan makes me nervous. I'm not crazy about

Ellika being on the squad, but I'm not comfortable hazing. It's just not me. So I'm planning to step aside and let the others do the "break her down bit by bit and make her life miserable" part. I'll do my part by ignoring her. If everyone just ignores her, it should make her miserable enough to leave the squad in a couple of weeks. I know if everyone ignored me, I'd be miserable.

"So, exactly how many rings are around Uranus?" Justin is asking Mrs. Pavlich.

"You'll have to open the book and see," answers Mrs. Pavlich.

"See what?" Justin asks.

"Uranus," she says.

"Ten to seven," says Lexie in a bored voice, crossing her legs. No one's really laughing anymore. The Uranus thing is stale now. Beth Ann and Lexie are passing notes, and Sloane is blowing on her fingernails. She's been touching up the tips of her French manicure with a bottle of white nail polish. I'm flipping through her magazine.

"My dad designed a high-tech photo telescope for NASA," says Compular, a.k.a. Ryan Blum. He's a compulsive liar.

"Did he design Pavlich's butt probe?" Justin asks.

"Naw, just yours, spazhole," Compular volleys back with a smile, completely unruffled. He never seems to care that no one believes his stories. If he were a dog, he'd be a happy little poodle: short, compact, dark curls, dimples. He's sitting in the row ahead of me, and I've caught him turning around to eye my legs a few times since class started. "For real, he patented it and everything," he says, turning to look at me. I nod, as if I believe him. It's easier than calling him a liar.

Griffin sneers, "No one cares, Compular." Griffin only opens his mouth to cut someone down. No one ever talks back to him, though. He's the type that might suddenly snap and pull a Columbine on all of us. He keeps getting suspended or expelled, but then his famous real-estate-developer dad sponsors a scholarship or chairs the annual benefit ball, and he's back at Beachwood. For all I know, his dad could be paying my tuition.

Which is hard to believe when you look at Griffin. His oily hair probably hasn't seen a comb for days and his wrinkled uniform polo is stained. I reflexively check my own shirt, even though I know it's spotless. I'm careful. I won't even let my mom put my uniform clothes in the dryer because I don't want them to get nubbly or faded. We hang-dry everything over our bathtub, Mom irons each piece until it's perfect, then we run a lint roller over it. Griffin's shirt has a hole in the seam, with threads hanging.

Only the rich can get away with looking that poor.

Lexie takes the nail polish from Sloane's desk, then gets up and sits in the empty seat right behind Ellika. Pavlich doesn't notice. Ellika is still wearing her hair in that stupid sideways ponytail.

Which is why it's easy for Lexie to paint across the back of her head.

At first she doesn't feel anything. Then she starts scratching, smearing it around. Snorts and silent laughing erupt from our back row. Her fingers are so stubby, they remind me of Viennese sausages, and her nails are bitten down to red nubs. She's getting white polish on her hands, but doesn't seem to notice. Or she's just pretending she doesn't notice. She has to smell it. The whole back row stinks of nail polish.

Both Beth Ann and Hunter switch seats with Lexie to have a turn with the nail polish. Ellika bites her lip and stares at her notebook. She doesn't move. Hunter paints polka dots. They look like giant dandruff flakes. She's very still. Hunter has a big smile on his face. He's really enjoying himself. He has an audience and he knows it.

I shouldn't be part of the audience. I should look at the board and actually try to learn something in this class, for once. And yet, like everyone else in the back of the room, I watch and wait to see what Ellika will do, how far this will go.

Hunter's hand snaps back when Ellika suddenly whips around to face him. "Please leave my hair alone." Her voice is really nasal, like she has a sinus problem.

"I'm not doing anything," says Hunter, covering the nail polish bottle with his hands. He looks at her like she's crazy.

"Yes, you are. You're, you're ..." She trails off.
"What?"
Ellika opens and closes her mouth a few times, as if

she wants to say something but it won't come out. Eventually, she manages to ask me, "Peyton, is there anything in my hair?" I guess Smellika feels comfortable asking me because we're locker neighbors.

My eyes jump to Lexie. She shakes her head no.

"No," I say casually. "I don't see anything."

Ellika scratches her head. She has to feel the nail polish. Some of it's on her fingers. But she just keeps scratching and then wrinkles up her nose. She really shouldn't do that. Her features are already squished into the middle of her face, like a reflection in a fun-house mirror.

"Are you sure?" she asks. There's something that looks like cream cheese in her teeth. Her eyes are big and bug-like, magnified behind glasses as thick as Dorkowitz's. "Are you sure?" she asks again with a big, wet sniff. I'm repulsed. I can't help it. She's the definition of disgusting.

"Did I stutter?" I snap, feeling rotten the second the words come out of my mouth.

But Lexie likes the way I said it, I can tell.

I have a feeling my strategy to ignore Ellika isn't going to be enough.

~ ~ ~

Lexie pushed Ellika down the stairs. Just now. I'm standing at the top of the staircase and it's crowded because Pavlich's class just ended and everybody is rushing around the halls to get to class, but I saw the whole thing. Lexie grabbed the back flap of Ellika's skort (no one, and I mean, no one, wears the skort) when she pushed her, and the button popped right off. Ellika fell pretty hard.

Now she's sprawled on the landing with the flap of her skort hanging open. The shorts under the flap are way too tight, giving her the worst wedgie I've ever seen. She's on all fours with her books and papers all over the place. Her orange glasses are hanging off one ear. The girl looks pathetic. I have an impulse to help her, so I start stepping down to pick up her stuff and see if she's okay.

But another impulse crawls out from under a rock somewhere inside me, stopping me in my tracks. I want to laugh at her. Maybe it's because Griffin yells out, "Smooth move, Captain She-tard!" A lot of people think that's funny, and that's probably part of the reason I want to laugh.

But mostly, it's the way she looks. She keeps trying to fasten the back flap of her skort over her big, square butt, but she can't find the button. And she's moving around scooping up her books and papers, while her sideways ponytail flops and waves like one of those goofy bobble heads. I feel sorry for her, but I want to laugh and point, too, like Griffin.

I don't act on either impulse. I just stand watching, a statue in the middle of all the kids swirling around me to get to class.

Lexie takes her time getting down to the landing. She holds out her hand and helps Ellika up. "Omigod, are you okay? Did someone push you?"

"Yeah, thanks," is all Ellika says, like it was no big deal.

She glances up at me when she says it.

3

A pair of white, jumbo-sized granny panties are hanging from a wire hanger hooked onto Ellika's locker vent. *Property Of Smellika Garret* is written across them in brown lipstick. I recognize the color: MAC Coconutty. The only color Lexie wears lately. The panties have to be from a gag store, like Spencer's. They're so huge you could cover a bean bag chair with them.

I see it before Ellika does because, lucky me, her locker is right next to mine. They do the lockers alphabetically, and Garret is right next to Grady. I just happen to be at school early today for a *Beacon* staff meeting. Right now no one is in the halls. Our meeting just ended, and only a few kids are in the building.

Her squat figure is bouncing toward me from the end of the hall. I race-walk away. I don't want to be around when she sees this, so I scramble down the stairs before she has a chance to sing out, "Hey there, Peyton," like she's been doing every morning since the assembly. I'm mystified as to how she found out my name so quickly. She's been trying to make conversation with me whenever we're at our lockers, even though I only give her one-word answers (in case someone from the squad is watching). Maya says I have a friendly face. It must be the freckles.

I get to AP English fifteen minutes early, a first for me. I've never been fifteen minutes early to anywhere. After English, the giant panties are gone and Dr. Johnson is patrolling the main hall in a plaid, bell-bottom ensemble. A security guard is with him.

Everyone on the squad is IMing and texting each other, wondering what Lexie will come up with next.

~ ~ ~

Please don't call on me, please don't call on me, I pray. Mr. Dharjami scans the room for victims to come up to the board and solve his three trig equations. The hand-wavers can't wait to get up there and show off, like Pinkie, of all people. It figures that the ditziest girl I know is some kind of Rain Man idiot savant in math. I, on the other hand, am your regular garden-variety idiot in math.

I stare at the floor, praying for it to open up and swallow me. Mr. Dharjami picks Pinkie and Jamar. Only one more to go. If he picks me, I won't know what to write up there and the whole class will see how clueless I am. I'll be exposed as the math moron that I am. *Please don't call on me, please don't call on me, pleeeeeeeease, God, don't let him call on me.*

I'll probably be saying the same silent prayer at Lexie's

house tomorrow night. Lexie sent us an evite for a squad sleepover so we can all brainstorm hazing ideas. So far I don't have any. The truth is, I'm a big chicken. I don't even know how I'm going to tell Maya I'm ditching her sleepover for Lexie's sleepover. I'm really stressed out.

The intercom buzzes and Rude Office Lady says, "Peyton Grady to the counselor's office." Hello, did I hear her cigarette-rasp correctly? "Peyton Grady needs to go see Mr. Pappas. Pronto. He's waiting." Yes! Yes! Waves of relief lift me up and float me out of the classroom. Saved by the intercom. Life is good again. Thank you, thank you, Rude Office Lady. Mr. Dharjami barely looks at me as he hands me the pass.

I take my time with a relaxing stroll on the way to the office. Forget making it pronto. Rude Office Lady says that to everyone. I run into Maya standing on a chair in the hallway, taping up posters with Carmen, Marisol, and some other student council kids.

Her face lights up when she sees me. Guilt, guilt, guilt. I still haven't thought of an excuse to get out of sleeping at her house. Worse, I'm dying to tell her about Lexie's sleepover and the whole Ellika thing. And I could use some advice on which nightshirt to bring.

"Hey, girlfriend," she says, handing me a roll of tape and stepping down off the chair. "How'd you get out of class?" I reach up and finish taping the poster. I don't need a chair.

"I got called in to see Mr. Pappas."

"You mean Mr. Papi," says Carmen.

"Yeah, Mr. Papi," echoes Marisol. Carmen and Marisol

have been best friends forever, like Maya and me. I've been cheering with them since freshman year.

"I don't think he's that cute," I tell them. Mr. Pappas is really young, like Coach Wisser. Some of the girls think he's gorgeous, but I don't see it. Maya pulls her eyebrows together, her way of asking, *Why do you have to see Mr. Pappas?* I shrug, flipping my palms upward.

I do have some idea, though. I forgot to show up for my advisory meeting last May. He's probably going to give me his "we're due for a talk" talk. Maya hands me one of her cell phones with an order: "Call me after."

I'm in between cell phones at the moment (read: I lost mine and Mom won't get me another one for a while because she thinks being phone-less will teach me a lesson about losing important things), but Maya has two. She convinced both sets of grandparents to buy her one for her birthday. Maya says there's nothing wrong with using your resources to get what you need. And why does Maya think she needs two cell phones, you may ask?

In case she ever loses one.

I swear, irony is my life. I slip her phone into my backpack. "Talk to you later."

That's when he shows up, stopping me in my tracks. His sandy-blond hair is falling into his eyes again. I want to brush it away with my fingers so badly. He's heading our way. I'm not going anywhere. Mr. Pappas can wait. He stops in front of us. I am dying.

"Hey, Marisol, is the sociology homework due today or tomorrow?" He asks, without even a glance in my direction.

"Tomorrow," she answers, not looking up. How can she just keep taping and not realize that a total god is speaking to her? If only I had registered for sociology this semester, it could be me telling him when his homework is due. Damn.

"Tomorrow? You're sure?"

"Yeah."

"Suh-weet. Hey, Marisol, who're your friends?" He's adjusting his belt buckle. It's very sexy how he's doing it.

"Von, where are you supposed to be right now?" Marisol crosses her arms at him like a teacher. *Shut up and introduce us,* I scream inside. He's just being polite though, because everybody knows everybody's name in our school. This proves that he is both a god and a gentleman.

"I don't know, like, study hall or something," he says, running his hand through his hair. We all know that study hall is only offered sixth period, not until after lunch, but no one says anything. Now he looks over at both Maya and me. "I'll introduce myself, since Marisol here is so rude. I'm Von Cohen." Even his name is beautiful.

"Oh, give it up, Von. You know Maya," says Marisol. Hello? Hello? Am I invisible, here?

He gives Maya's body a quick once-over from under his wisps of hair. "Yeah, the whole school knows you, Maya. You were on, like, every page of the yearbook last year." She's wearing the navy uniform polo dress. It's supposed to hang loosely but it's snug on Maya's curves, and she looks voluptuous and amazing in it. I hate her right now.

"Whassup?" He asks her.

"Not much. Do you know Peyton?" I love her right now.

"Hi." I smile big, my lips quivering because I'm so nervous. I'm looking right into his green eyes. They're the same olive color as mine. Who knew? He's taller than me, a rare and wonderful sight to behold. I must remember to breathe.

"What's up?"

"Nothing," I reply, bursting with razor-sharp wit.

"Aren't you a cheerleader?" He asks.

"Yeah." *Think of something to say, Peyton.* "We're, uh, doing a pep rally tomorrow at the end of the day."

"Nice. We'll get out of eighth period." He lifts up his palm to high five me. I stare at it. It takes a second for me to slap him back. I touched him. Omigod. I have to smell my hand later.

"Hey there, Peyton." It's Ellika. She's headed this way. No way, not now. She will not, cannot destroy this moment. I don't answer. I refuse to answer and ruin my first and possibly only conversation with the god of my dreams.

"Hey there, Peyton." She's closer. Von and I are finally at the eye-contact, face-to-face, possible flirting stage, and *now* is when Ellika decides to show up?

This cannot be happening.

Von turns around and sees her. He winces. "Whoa, she ain't easy on the eyes, your buddy over there."

"She's not my buddy," I say. "She just, her locker's next to mine."

"Hey there, Peyton. Will you be at practice today?" She's

standing right next to me now. I look at Maya for some clues, but she's as blank as me. Carmen and Marisol squinch up their faces in disgust, the way I do when I see road kill on Route 441.

"Yeah, I'll be there," I mumble, barely meeting her eyes. Ellika just stands there. We all just stand there. Talk about awkward.

"Okay, well, I'm off," says Von, backing away. "Later, ladies." I watch him walk away, wanting to kick a locker, wanting to kick Ellika.

"I gotta go, too," she says. "I'm supposed to meet my mom out front. Doctor's appointment. Did you get my candy gram?"

I'm unable to speak.

"I think they deliver them after lunch. You'll get it later." She faces Carmen and Marisol. "The whole squad will get one." And then she's back to me. "Anyway, I have to go see my ophthalmologist. Your eyes are so green. Are they contacts?"

I shake my head no.

"Oh. I thought your eyes were fake. My mom wants me to wear contacts, but I can't put my finger in my eye. I've tried it, and I just can't. Uh-oh, look at the time. I better go. See you guys later." She thumps away with that weird, bouncy waddle, her toes pointing outward at ten to two, ten to two, ten to two.

"Great. Thanks for all the info," I say after she's far enough away. "Why does she always talk to me? Always me, no one else. Why?"

"Who knows?" says Maya. "She sure has diarrhea of the mouth, though."

"And constipation of the brain," says Marisol. She and Carmen crack up.

I'm not laughing. "Could she be any more annoying? I mean, did she really have to interrupt us like that? What a pain in the ass." I don't add that she destroyed my Von moment. I'm seething. I can't believe she had to show up now, of all times. Lexie's right. She deserves to be called Smellika. I want to vent my frustration with Maya and discuss how much I want him, but not in front of Carmen and Marisol. They're high up on the gossip chain.

"I just can't believe she's on the squad with us," says Carmen. "All her *dinero* doesn't mean jack. She's gonna make us look retarded."

"Don't let Lexie hear you say that," warns Marisol.

"Forget about her and your precious squad," Maya says. "Did you see the way he was looking at you, Pey? I think he likes you."

Too late to keep my crush a secret now. I toss my head in Carmen and Marisol's direction and give Maya my *thanks a lot* smirk. "Looking at me what way? You're insane in the membrane. I gotta go. I am so late."

"Wait," Maya says. "You have to ask him to the dance."

"What dance?" I ask. Maya reaches up and lightly presses her hands on each side of my face before twisting my head to read the poster I taped. I hadn't paid attention before. Bold blue letters scream out, *Sadie Hawkins Dance!*

Friday, September 15. Don't pass the night by, Go out and grab your guy! There's a drawing of a girl in overalls throwing a lasso over a boy.

"This looks dumb," I say without thinking.

"It's not dumb," Carmen and Marisol sing at the same time.

"Peyton, it was my idea," says Maya in a pissy way.

"Sorry. I guess the hillbilly thing just hits a little too close to home," I backpedal. She knows where my mom is from.

"It's girls ask boys, and you have to ask Von," she insists. "You have to, Pey."

"No way. I could never."

"Personally, I thought he was into you," says Marisol.

Carmen's nodding her head. "Definitely. You should ask him. I've asked a guy out before. It's no big."

"You're all whacked." I'm turning pink. I feel it. "Seriously, I have to go." I leave before the blushing gets worse. I couldn't possibly ask him out. I've barely said two words to him. He's probably forgotten all about me by now.

But what an amazing dream come true it would be if I asked him and he said yes. It would be my very first date ever. I could finally join the rest of the female teen population by actually having a date. And with the hottest guy in school! In my opinion, anyway. I'm lightheaded just thinking about it.

I replay my mental DVD of our brief but beautiful conversation all the way to Mr. Pappas' office.

4

"Hey, Mr. Pappas."

"Peyton! What took you so long? I was beginning to think you were blowing me off again."

"Sorry."

"I'm going to get right down to business, okay? Mr. Dharjami is concerned about your comprehension of trigonometry."

"What comprehension?"

"Exactly."

"But it's only the first week of school. I can improve, Mr. Pappas. I will improve." I have no idea how I will do this.

"Of course you will. You're a bright kid and a hard worker."

"So tell Mr. Dharjami not to be so intense." Oh, yeah, and could you tell him never, ever to call on me while you're at it?

"That would be like telling the wind not to blow. Besides, math has always been your weak area." Maybe it's the teachers who are weak. I bet he never considered that. "Look, you got a C- in Algebra and a D in Geometry for your final quarter last year. Frankly, I'm concerned about your scholarship."

I'm concerned about it, too. I swallow back the lump in my throat. I won't cry, no matter what. "It was a D+. And I've always gotten As in AP English and in journalism and PE. Oh, and I got a B+ in biology." Thanks to Dorkowitz. "I'm a good student."

"Overall, yes. But I don't want to see your GPA decline. You got a C in Spanish II last spring." Can I help it if I don't *hablo* so well? "And you only got a C- in Domestic Arts. How could you get a C- in Domestic Arts?"

"You know, making a doily is really hard." He grins. Maybe he is kind of hot, for a teacher. "You know, the Martha thing is over. That class shouldn't even be offered."

"That may be, but it brought down your average. You still have to maintain a 3.3 to keep your scholarship."

"What about my extracurriculars? I cheer on varsity now and I'm 'Last Look' writer for the *Beacon*."

"That's great, but those don't affect your GPA. Generally speaking, you're a good student. You just had a little sophomore slump. If it wasn't for your scholarship, I wouldn't be too worried, but I'd be lying if I said that your slump won't affect your eligibility for financial aid."

I've been at this school since I was five years old. My

eyes sting. "Peyton, you're an asset to Beachwood. We'd hate to lose you." I step on my foot, hard. I will not cry. "And this year counts the most, you know. College applications go out next year."

"I know."

"I think we need to implement a strategy now for success, before the semester is over and you're drowning even deeper in trig. You need to pull up your grades."

"I agree. I'll do whatever it takes."

"That's the spirit."

"So, what do you suggest?"

"Well, first of all, you need a tutor. Once a week, minimum."

"Okay. How do I get one?"

"I can recommend a few for you to call."

"Does it cost anything?"

"Most tutors charge forty to sixty an hour."

"Dollars? Or cents? Because I don't have forty dollars a week." My eyes are stinging again. I dig my heel deeper. I'll probably be limping out of here.

"I thought you might say that. We can get a top math student to do it for community service. I'll talk to Mr. Dharjami and set that up. I have a good one in mind."

"Who?"

"Ryan Blum. Do you know him?"

"Compular? You're kidding, right?"

"I don't believe I am. He's an exceptionally talented student."

"And he'll do it for free?"

"Yes."

"I guess I don't have a choice. I'll take him."

"Good. Now, let's do what we can to pull up the elective grades. Stick with courses you can ace."

"Well, I'm taking astronomy."

"Excellent. No problem there." Even Mr. Pappas knows what a goof-off class it is.

"And I'm taking humanities."

"Hmmm, there's still time to drop that one. Mrs. Lowe doesn't give As very often."

"How about sociology? I know I could ace sociology. I'm, like, really interested in it." Von, here I come.

"Mmmm, I don't think so. That course is full."

"Come on, Mr. Pappas. Can't you squeeze me in? I know I could ace it."

"I wish I could, but no can do." Why is my life so cursed? Why am I doomed to a schedule without Von in it? "You know, Peyton, with your background, I'm surprised you haven't taken drama."

"With Dr. Giles? I don't think so." She gives me the willies. Her shoulders are wider than most NFL linebackers'.

"But your father's an actor. In New York, right?"

"Yeah. An out-of-work one in New York, for two years now. That's the whole reason I need financial aid to stay at Beachwood. He can't even make child support and alimony payments, let alone my tuition. My mother's scared to death I'll be interested in drama. She'll never let me take it."

"I'll call and convince her, don't worry. I'm pretty good with parents, if I do say so myself. Funny, I thought she was an actress, too."

"A model. Ex-model, actually. Now she's a makeup artist. Not that she's curling J.Lo's eyelashes or anything. She works at Bloomingdale's, at the Chanel counter." Now Mr. Pappas knows more about me than anyone else in the whole school does, except for Maya. It feels weird telling him all this stuff.

"So then you should feel right at home on the stage."

"Nope, I'm missing that gene."

"But you perform for crowds when you're cheering."

"Yeah, but that's different. I'm not alone out there."

"You should take drama, Peyton. It's very possible to get an A in that class, which is what you need right now to keep your scholarship.

"What if I have no talent? I've never tried out for any plays."

"You can do stage crew. Just be enthusiastic and show up ready to work. You'll get an A for effort if you try hard enough."

"I'll try harder than anybody there."

"Good."

~ ~ ~

I dial Maya's other cell phone.

"Hello?"

"Hi."

"Where are you?"

"Walking to my locker. Where are you?"

"Still hanging posters. What did Pappas say?"

"I have to get a tutor for trig and you'll never guess who it is."

"Who?"

"Compular!"

"Aaaaaaaaaaaahhhhh! No way."

"Way."

"No way."

"Way."

"What is he, some kind of math genius?"

"Apparently. He's been checking me out lately, too."

"Compular? Congrats, you dweeb magnet."

"Thanks. Plus I have to take Giles' Drama I class. To boost my GPA. I'll be the only junior, I'm sure."

"Not the only one, girlfriend."

"You too?"

"Hooray, we have a class together."

"I'm so happy."

"You have to ask Von, Pey. The way he introduced himself was like, epic. You so have to ask him."

"I know. I'm thinking about it."

"Guess what? I asked somebody to the dance right after you left."

"What? Without consulting me first? Who?"

"Jamar."

"Really? What will your parents say?"

"Because he's African American? They can hardly complain about that."

"No, because he's not Jewish." The only boyfriends Maya ever had were Dave Berman and Marcus Fishbein.

"Hey, my shrink says I have to get in touch with the black side of my identity. So I figure I should start by going out with Jamar."

I scream with joy to show my support. "Way to go, Maya-mooch. He's really hot. How did you ask him?"

"I'll tell you tomorrow night. Let's have an eighties marathon—I rented your favorites, *Pretty in Pink* and *Sixteen Candles*. Your mom looks just like Molly Ringwald."

I take a deep breath and plunge right in. The moment of deception has arrived. "I can't come, girlfriend. I'm so sorry. I totally forgot to tell you."

"What? Please say you're not serious."

"See, my mom's been working late for two weeks and she feels like she hasn't spent any time with me. She's off tomorrow tonight and she's guilting me into a mother-daughter bonding night." Why am I talking so fast? "She's being a real pain. I'm so sorry," I lie.

"Oh."

"You know I'd rather be at your place," I lie some more.

"I even stocked up on Raisinets and Snow Caps. I'll have to watch all those movies by myself now." Her voice is very small.

"Next Friday, for sure. I promise, promise, promise."

"You better. And call me tonight after practice. I want to hear how it went with Ellika."

"You mean Smellika."

5

She can't even touch her toes. We're bending and twisting like rubber bands, and she's grunting over a simple stretch. Our Soffe gym shorts and layered tanks are trendy and cute. Her clothes are all wrong. It's obvious she made an attempt to get it right, wearing drawstring sweatpants and an Abercrombie and Fitch T-shirt. But the sweats are a size too small, and we can all see craters of cellulite below thick panty lines. Her shirt is way too big, more like something you'd wear for a sleepover, not cheer practice. This poor girl is so out of place, it's like having a penguin waddling around with us.

The candy grams came during eighth period. Everyone on the squad got a baggie of Hershey's Kisses with a note that said, "Looking forward to being part of the team!" Smellika asked a few of us if we got them, but we all played dumb, as in: "What candy gram? I didn't get any candy gram." Now she keeps trying out a small smile on each of us, hoping someone will respond a little. She's trying so hard, it's pathetic. She doesn't understand that the more she tries, the more she's asking for it.

Ellika Garret doesn't know what she's up against. We're a united front. We ignore her, as directed. And just like when I watched Lexie send her crashing down the stairs, I feel sorry for her, but I can't stand her either. Pity and disgust are all rolled into one confusing lump every time I look at her.

"Okay, that's enough of a warm-up," Lexie says. "We need to get our timing down on the pep rally routine, or else we'll be running into each other during transitions tomorrow. Let's line up."

Smellika waves the remote for the sound system. "Should I hit play?" She's in charge of cuing our music, pretty much all she's good for at this point. Juretha tried to teach her some of the dance section, but she's hopeless. There isn't one strand of athletic DNA anywhere in her body. Not to mention rhythm. It's such an insult to the rest of us who've earned the right to be here, who have some talent to offer the squad.

Lexie pretends not to see her waving the remote around. Smellika can't take a hint. "Lexie, should I hit play? Lexie? Lexie?"

"Jesus Christ, did I *tell you* to hit play? No. No, I did not. What part of 'I'll tell you when to hit play' don't you understand?"

"Sorry." Smellika sinks into the bleachers, probably hoping to blend in with the wood.

We line up behind the door and tumble across the gym until we get to our marks. Being so tall, tumbling is not my forte. I kind of fake it, doing cartwheels and round-offs. If I mess up, I stop and do a jump. Sloane, Beth Ann, Raquel and Devin are the gymnasts. They can pick up speed in no time and do back handsprings across the length of an entire court. Devin can even do a whip back, which looks like a back handspring but no hands touch the floor.

We all have at least one strength. I'm best at basing and dancing. Carmen and Marisol are good dancers, too, adding a lot of hot moves to everything. "Five, six, seven, eight," Lexie calls, and we go into our routine. Even with no music, I love, love, *love* to dance.

Next comes the cheer: "Come on, come on, Sharks! Let's go, Let's fight, We've got the bite, Gonna win tonight, S-H-A-R-K-S. GO SHARKS GO!" Our moves are sharp and we hit it perfectly. Kaitlyn and Shawntay are insanely loud, bursting with energy. They're always in the front of a formation, on either side of Lexie.

When it's time for our pyramid, Pinkie, our number one flyer, is on top. She dismounts in a perfect toe-touch—springing out into a V-split and touching her toes in midair before landing. She's fearless and tiny and makes it look easy, but, believe me, there have been falls when I thought Pinkie was a goner. We can usually hear her giggling for no reason up there. Pinkie definitely puts the ding in cheerleading.

Lexie's an amazing flyer too, and she writes and choreographs a lot of our cheers. She actually does everything well, which is why she's captain. Juretha's an awesome choreographer and a dedicated cheer-natic. She and Lexie make up all the routines together. As far as varsity squads go, the twelve of us rock. Now what are we supposed to do with an odd-girl-out who has no skills whatsoever?

We practice it a few times with the music, until Coach Wisser drops by the gym to watch. She only stays about twenty minutes at every practice, just pops in to give us pointers, then takes off, leaving Lexie in charge of us. I'm pretty sure it's against the rules.

But rules are for ordinary people, not Lexie.

Coach Wisser is here now, so we're forced pull Smellika off the bench and include her. "I think Ellika can try basing for a simple lift, don't you, Peyton?" Coach Wisser asks me. "Think you can partner with her for a double base thigh stand?" I don't think Smellika can partner with a two-year-old for a piggyback ride, but what am I supposed to say, no?

A thigh stand is easy to base. It's just two bases facing each other, stepping back into a lunge, while a flyer steps onto the upper thigh pocket of each base and stands, lifting her arms up into a high V. I show Smellika how the toes on her straight leg should be pointing toward the audience, how the knee on the bent leg needs to be directly above the ankle. Pinkie steps up onto both of us, and I hold the front of her foot and the back of her knee for support. "Hold her foot like me," I tell Smellika, and she copies me. Juretha, spotting behind us, holds Pinkie lightly around the waist.

As far as stunts go, this is as basic as it gets, but Smellika can't handle it. It's sad. She's struggling to keep her back leg locked, and she keeps sniffing. Her glasses are sliding down her nose. They're about to fall off her face. "Better get those contacts," I tell her. "And keep your chest up, square your shoulders. It'll help you with balance." We do it a few times so Pinkie can practice her dismount.

Smellika's legs are shaking. I'm afraid she's going to collapse with Pinkie on top of us. But she somehow forgets that Pinkie is there, balancing a foot on her. Without warning, Smellika stands up, saying, "Um, I need to blow my nose."

And there goes Pinkie, reeling backward, missing Juretha, crashing onto the blue mat. "What the—*aaaah*, you moron!" Pinkie screams. But half a sec later, she pops up like a jack-in-the-box. "I'm okay, I'm okay, I'm okay," she calls out, her rat-a-tat-tat giggle going a mile a minute.

Smellika starts to apologize. "Omigod, Pinkie, I'm—"

"Shut up!" Lexie shouts. Smellika freezes. We all do. Lexie turns to Coach Wisser. "Laura, could you please deal with her? We can't work with a damn health hazard."

Any other student would get a demerit for calling Coach Wisser "Laura," but Coach Wisser just nods at Lexie. "Come with me, Ellika. We need to go over some safety rules and practice support positions. Maybe we need to start you off as a spotter. I can't have you, or anybody, getting hurt." To Lexie, she says quietly, "You need to chill, okay?" The coach and Lexie have a close bond. I've heard rumors that they go shopping together.

All of us watch Smellika follow Coach Wisser to a corner of the room. She never takes her eyes off the floor.

Lexie takes control again. "Skip the two-one. Let's do the shark shake. We're not nailing it yet, and it's got to be solid right out of the gate. Places, come on, guys." She waits and then shouts, "Ready!"

We shout back, "Okay!" with a sharp clap. We practice it a few times, getting the moves really sharp and synchronized. Coach Wisser is showing Smellika some simple dance steps, but the girl is seriously uncoordinated. When we line up for another run-through, we notice the JV girls watching the Smellika sideshow instead of practicing their routine. They cover their mouths with their hands, making comments we can't hear. A few snorts echo across the room.

"They're dissing us," Lexie says. "How dare they." She orders them to buy us water bottles from the vending machines. I'm so glad I'm not on JV anymore. Most kids at school don't even know who the JV cheerleaders are. They don't get to wear their cheer uniforms to school on game days, just for the occasional pep rally. At Beachwood, you haven't made it until you've made it onto varsity.

After Coach Wisser leaves, Lexie calls for a ten minute break while the JV squad brings us our waters. "I changed my mind," Lexie says to a freshman girl offering her a bottle. "Bring me a Diet Coke. And a lemon slice to go with it."

The girl's forehead scrunches up with worry. "But where am I going to find—"

"I guess you'll have to figure it out, won't you?" Lexie says with a shrug. "And hurry up." The girl runs off.

I sit on the floor and press the cool bottle to my sweaty

face. I love the way it feels. Lexie and Beth Ann plunk themselves down on either side of me, which is pretty unusual. They typically group off with Sloane and Devin during breaks.

"I'm all packed for your sleepover tomorrow," I say to Lexie.

"Yeah, it'll be fun. We'll order in after the game. Chinese okay with you, Prairie Girl?" Lexie started calling me Prairie Girl when I made varsity. I love it. I think I'm the only one she gave a nickname to. She says I remind her of the girl in that seventies show, *Little House on the Prairie*. I watched the Hallmark channel all summer trying to see a resemblance.

"Sure. I love Chinese," I say. She doesn't need to know that my mom's been bringing home Takee-Outee all week and I'm actually sick of Chinese at the moment. The freshman girl shows up all breathless, handing Lexie a Diet Coke and a plastic cup with two slices of lemon perched on the rim.

"The cafeteria was closed, but they let me in to get you your lemon," she says, panting. Lexie takes the cup and soda and waves her away like a fly.

The three of us watch Smellika guzzle her water. "My dog sucks it down like that," says Beth Ann. Lexie makes barfing motions and lies down on her belly. She props herself up on her elbows, facing me. "Uch, I can't look at that retard anymore."

"Me either," I agree, twisting my torso. My lower back aches from bending over for the last twenty minutes. I spread my legs into a V-split, reaching out my arms and pressing my chest into the floor. It's a good stretch for the lower back.

Lexie snaps open her soda and whistles. "Wow, check out the long, lean legs on you, Peyton. They're smokin'."

"I'm jealous," Beth Ann adds.

"Yeah, right," I answer. Those two being jealous of me is beyond ridiculous. It's just their opener for the *Compliment Your Body* game they've started. It's something girls do sometimes. Now it's my turn.

I sit up, glance at Beth Ann's double D's and sigh, "If I had your boobs, we could make the perfect body together."

She must be thinking what I'm thinking, that the perfect body is lying next to us. Lexie's curves are perfectly proportioned, every girl's impossible goal, like a Barbie or a fembot. Beth Ann is constantly losing ten pounds or gaining it back. Most of those ten pounds are in her chest. "You don't want them this big. I tried on one of those cute little tanks at Hollister and it was so tight, I looked totally trailer park. You're so lucky, you have no idea. You can buy anything."

Lucky me, I can buy anything? Sure can, Beth Ann, or could, if it wasn't for that little lack-of-money problem ... but, hey, don't worry your pretty little diamond-earrings-wearing head about it ... "At least you can fill out a tank top."

"I'd rather have your thin thighs."

"I'd rather have your cleavage."

"Boobs are overrated."

"Not when you don't have any."

She doesn't answer. Game over. We sip our water quietly for a minute. Usually, practice is fun with a lot of horsing around. Today the whole squad is quiet.

At some point, Justin and Hunter and some of the other guys from the football team will show up at our practice after theirs is over. Some stay to watch us from the bleachers, some just talk and flirt for a few minutes. Others strut toward the boys' locker room, casually ripping off their jerseys and pads without breaking stride, flashing their abs and shoulders for our viewing pleasure in a *quién es más macho* contest.

Smellika clumps past us to wait her turn at the water fountain. Devin is ahead of her, refilling her bottle. She looks over at Lexie, plugs her nose and rolls back her eyes, as if she's passing out from Smellika's b.o. Smellika stares straight ahead, pretending she doesn't see what Devin is doing.

I can't figure out why she's putting herself through all this abuse, why she's choosing to take it. Why does Ellika Garret, possibly one of the richest kids in Florida, want to stick around where she's not wanted, getting dumped on every minute? She could find other extracurriculars with kids like Dorkowitz, kids more like herself. It's only the first week of school. She could make a clean getaway from Lexie and all of us, start over, get her name back. I just don't get it.

"Isn't your locker next to Smellika's?" Lexie asks me, pulling me out from inside my head. I nod, taking a sip from my bottle. She moves closer to me. "Make sure you get rid of her uniform before the pep rally tomorrow."

"What?"

"Steal her uniform."

I giggle. That would be a good one. Which reminds me. "I saw that on an old *Buffy the Vampire Slayer* once. Buffy's sister stole Buffy's cheerleading uniform and cut it up into little pieces. Did you ever see that episode?"

Lexie isn't smiling. Her chocolate eyes are cold. "No."

My grin fades. "You really want me to steal her uniform?"

"Yeah. I really do."

OMIGOD.

I thought she was joking.

"But how? I mean, how can I steal it? I don't know her locker combination."

"You're smart. You'll think of something."

I don't know where she got the impression I'm smart about stuff like this, but she's highly mistaken. Highly. "What if she sees me?"

Lexie shrugs. "Just make sure her uniform disappears. Tomorrow." I stare at her, trying to think of a good excuse as to why I cannot possibly steal Smellika's uniform, other than the fact that I'm scared of getting in trouble, as well as the fact that I don't have the slightest idea how to steal someone's stuff.

"This is about the squad, Peyton."

Beth Ann nods. "We need you. Your locker is right next to hers. You're the only one who can do it. You, um ..." Her eyes drift over to Lexie.

"You look so innocent," Lexie finishes for her. "No one would ever suspect you."

"Right, that's it," Beth Ann says as if she just remembered her line in a script. "You're super-duper innocent looking."

Beth Ann is a terrible actress. This *is* some kind of script they're following. They totally sound like some rehearsed, corny, make-believe show.

But it's not TV. It's real life. And there's no way out.

Lexie is clenching her jaw, waiting for me to say something. Her face is hard. "Peyton, this is not about you, it's about all of us. Remember that." Then instantly, like she's flicked on some internal light switch, every inch of her face softens. She puts her arm around my shoulder. I smell the musk from her deodorant. "Come on, Prairie Girl. You can do it."

I should be flattered that they're depending on me, that they trust me to get it done. And I am, in a way. It's twisted, but come on, out of the whole squad, Lexie picked *me* to do the deed. Except why does it have to be stealing? Why couldn't I be chosen for something else?

"Tomorrow?" I ask, as if I have to check my busy schedule to see if I can fit in a robbery. They both nod. Damn that alphabetical locker system. This is so huge, I wish I could tell Maya. But I can't. She'd never understand. "No problem." I sip my water. Maybe it'll wash away the stress gnawing at my insides. "No problem at all."

How in hell am I going to pull this off?

6

It's easier than I thought.

"Shoot, I left my jump drive in the computer lab. Be right back," Smellika says, leaving her locker door wide open. Her gym bag is hanging on the hook. I don't think, I just do it. It takes all of ten seconds to unzip the bag, grab her uniform, stuff it into my bag, and zip hers back up. My hands shake the whole time.

I meet Lexie in the girls bathroom behind the cafetorium. No one ever goes there. She snuffs out her cigarette in the sink when I walk in. I hand over Smellika's clothes. Lexie holds them up before shoving everything in a plastic bag and throwing it all in the garbage. I wait for her to say, "good job, Peyton," or "I knew I could count on you," but she says, "Jesus Christ, I didn't know they made uniforms that huge."

~ ~ ~

We're putting barrettes in our hair, sparkle gel on our eyelids, and lotion on our legs. Sloane is spraying her butt with Firm Grip, a spray that football players use to make the ball stick to their hands when they catch it. We use it to make our spankies stick to our skin so they don't ride up in the back.

"Anybody need some?" Sloane asks, holding the can up. I use it and pass it on to Devin. Lexie is throwing handfuls of glitter in the air, showering us with silver dust. She says she wants us to shine out there. We're all nervous, but the mood is fun. This is the part I love, the part that feels like I'm in a special club. We look so good in our gold and white varsity uniforms. The skirts flare out in just the right way, and our spankies have little sequined sharks sewn on the rear.

Everyone's pumped up about the rally and the game, excited for the whole school to see us. There's only one thing getting in the way of my personal excitement. Smellika is nowhere in sight. She never even showed up. That's what was supposed to happen, the whole reason I stole her uniform, but I keep imagining how she must have opened her gym bag earlier and realized it was gone. I hope it didn't make her cry. I know I did it for the good of the squad, but I feel crappy about it just the same.

"Okay, guys, we're on in fifteen," says Lexie. "Remember, focus and visualize. Let's go stretch." We chant, "Let's get fired up," all the way to the gym.

Once we walk into the lobby of the GAF, the scene

smacks us quiet like we've been doused with a bucket of Gatorade. Smellika, Coach Wisser, and another woman are in an intense conversation. We get dead silent. They're standing by the door talking quietly, practically whispering. Smellika's eyes are glued to the floor. My heart is jumping out of my rib cage, pounding my ears.

Do they know I stole her uniform? Did Smellika figure it out? Am I going to get suspended? Will they call my mom? She'd kill me if I ever got suspended. Oh God, maybe I'll even get arrested. Isn't stealing someone's personal property a felony or a misdemeanor or something? It's definitely against the law. What if I have to go to juvie? That's jail. Jail for kids.

Must. Stay. Calm.

I can only hear bits and pieces of what they're saying. "Ellika's told me . . . such a warm welcome from the girls."

" . . . don't know how I lost it . . . could have sworn it was in my bag . . ."

" . . . so sorry she can't find it . . . can't participate without the uniform . . ." The GAF is filling up with kids heading into the gym, getting really loud. I stretch out like everyone else, straining to hear. Smellika is saying she lost her uniform. She actually thinks she lost it. How could that be?

Who cares? I'm off the hook. I'm getting away with it. Scot free. Incredible. Unbelievable. I am beyond relieved. I would never have survived in juvie. And now my mom will never know I committed theft.

The famous Mrs. Garret is nothing like I'd imagined.

I'd always assumed she'd be a typical Boca socialite decked out in designer tennis clothes, diamonds, and a Gucci bag. But she's exactly the opposite, old and plain. She could even pass for a grandmother. There's a reddish, hair-sprayed puff sitting on her head that looks like a rusty Brillo pad.

"Our little girl would lose her head if it wasn't attached to her neck... had to reschedule a fundraising meeting to come today..."

Lexie isn't stretching like the rest of us. She's leaning her hip against the wall, arms crossed, watching the discussion. After a few seconds, she throws her shoulders back and goes over to them, flashing a 2,000-watt smile.

"Hi. You must be Ellika's mother," she says with all the smooth confidence of somebody ultra-important, like a congresswoman or Oprah. "I just wanted to introduce myself. I'm Lexie Court, squad captain." Mrs. Garret shakes her hand. I'm staring openly, now. We all are, even Smellika. Forget stretching. Lexie's up to something.

"Nice to meet you, Lexie. By any chance, are you Bunny Court's daughter?"

Lexie's smile loses its juice for a second, but she turns it back on. "Yes, I am. How do you know Mother, if you don't mind my asking?"

"Not at all. We were co-chairs for a ballet benefit, years ago. I used to run into her from time to time, committee work and all that. How is Bunny these days?"

"Very well, thank you." Some of Lexie's face muscles

are twitching. "Uh, anyway, I just wanted to say hello and tell you how happy we are to have Ellika on the squad."

It's amazing to watch Lexie's mouth saying one thing while her eyes are saying just the opposite. They've turned into slits, burning a hole into Smellika's face. Smellika steps closer to her mother. She looks petrified. If she figures anything out about her uniform disappearance, Lexie's death-dealing eyes are making it clear she better keep her mouth shut.

"How nice of you to say so, Lexie." Mrs. Garret is buying Lexie's act, hook, line, and sinker. It's almost embarrassing. "Ellika's father and I always thought cheerleading would be perfect for her, with her sunny personality." She stops to put her arm around her daughter. "And she's just delighted to be part of your team."

"Oh, the pleasure is all ours, Mrs. Garret," Lexie gushes, like a pro. I know some kids my age who can talk to adults like an equal; Maya can do that. But Lexie's the only one I know who talks to adults like she's *above* them. Why she's putting on this display for Smellika's mother is a mystery.

Coach Wisser opens the door of the practice room. "Mrs. Garret, I'm so sorry, but you'll have to excuse us. The girls have a performance now. We'll order a new uniform for Ellika ASAP."

"Of course, of course. Thank you for your time. And Lexie, do give my regards to your mother."

Lexie grants Mrs. Garret a royal wave. "I will." She walks toward us and whispers "not."

"What was up with all that?" Beth Ann asks Lexie. We're waiting in the hall by the gym door for our cue.

"Trust me." Lexie checks the clasp on her Tiffany bracelet. "I know what I'm doing." JV is lining up in front of us. They go on first. The band has already started the rally by leading the student body in the school song. Our band bites and no one is singing, except for a few kids who change all the words to make it dirty.

"But what are you doing, exactly?" Sloane asks, leaning close to Lexie with her hands on her hips. She whispers, "I thought we wanted to kick her off the squad, not roll out the red carpet."

Lexie stabs a finger in Sloane's face. "Are you questioning me?"

Sloane backs away, holding up her hands as if Lexie's finger is loaded. "No, no, of course not. I'm sorry. I guess I just don't get it."

Lexie glances at all of us before leaning in close to Sloane to answer her. "Look, we have to make sure it looks like Smellika leaves because she wants to, like we did everything we could for her, but she still decided to drop out. And not, I repeat, *not* because we did anything wrong." She pauses. "Any more questions?" We shake our heads.

"Good. Because I just bought us a little extra insurance by making nice. I want to avoid suspicion. It's all part of the plan. *Comprendez moi* now, Sloane?" Sloane nods and

Lexie does an about-face, slapping Sloane's forehead with her pony-tail. She makes a beeline for Hunter, who's lining up with the rest of the football team for their entrance onto the court.

I get it now, too. I swear, Lexie is a genius. Who else would think of sucking up to the enemy? So smart. No wonder she's applying to Harvard.

Carmen and Marisol are practicing the dance section where we shout, "shark shake!" They call that move the booty bomb. Juretha joins in, so I do too. We're all having fun, shaking our butts and everything, when we hear Mrs. Garret call out, "Good luck, girls."

We freeze. She's walking out of the ladies' room with Smellika. As they make their way to the exit, Smellika looks straight at me. I stop breathing. Our eyes lock. Does my face give me away? Is it saying I stole her uniform? Does she know? I knew that whole "I don't know how I lost it" stuff was too good to be true.

She and her mother walk out through the main exit, the one that has *Garret Athletic Facility* embossed on a huge sign above the door. I breathe again.

"I'd like to know who shellacked Granny Garret's hair," says Devin, to the hoots and claps of the squad. A lot of girls dance the shark shake booty bomb again and I join in, glad to forget what I did to Smellika, glad to loosen up and get goofy. I don't even notice that Von is standing next to us, enjoying the show. We all see him at the same time and let out girly screams, embarrassed. I'm the most embarrassed one of all. My face is so hot, it must be strawberry.

"You want some fries with those shakes?" He asks. It's the oldest joke in the world, but I throw my head back and laugh and laugh and laugh. I want him to think I'm so fun, so whimsical, so playful that he can't help but be drawn to me and my *joie de vivre*. I was so busy worrying about Smellika that I didn't even see him. I can't believe it.

"Shut up, Von," says Marisol, slapping him on the arm. "Get in the gym. You're late."

He pushes the gym door open. He's getting away and I didn't even say anything. I spot Lexie and Beth Ann with Hunter and Justin. Flirting comes so easily to them, like breathing. I open my mouth to at least say hi before the door closes when, miracle of miracles, Von beats me to it. "Hey, Peyton cheerleader." He's holding the door open, about to go in.

"Hey," I hear myself answer. He goes into the gym. He singled me out. Me. Out of everybody. I must be dreaming.

Marisol and Carmen start buzzing. "Ask him, ask him, when are you going to ask him to Sadie's?" I just shrug. JV finishes their routine and our cue comes on. Lexie shouts, "Sell it! Smiles!" Coach Wisser holds the door open so we can get a running start before we cartwheel and backflip across the gym.

The crowd cheers. Some kids are too cool to cheer, mostly the anti-cliques. I spot Von in the front row right away. He's sitting with his crew of skater friends. It could be my imagination, but it seems as if he's only watching me.

Even if he isn't, I dance just for him. I let go and get totally into the music, dancing full out, like I do when I'm alone. I'm so glad our dance section comes before the cheer. When the booty bomb part starts, I turn it on even more, really working it.

He *is* staring at me. He is *totally* staring at me. I'm not imagining it. And I can tell he likes what he sees. My adrenaline is pumping, my hair is whipping around my face, and there's no better feeling than this.

When I'm dancing, it's pure freedom, like nothing else matters, not even Smellika or my F on today's trig quiz or my scholarship or anything. We hit our routine perfectly, too, landing every stunt. The whole squad is full of spirit, loud and synchronized. I am so proud of us.

We finish and the crowd goes wild, especially Von. I love him even more for that. We do a few more jumps and tumble off to stand right in front of the bleachers. I would give positively anything—my right arm or my virginity or my entire CD collection—to be standing in front of his section, but due to the practical joke that is my life, I'm on the other side.

I have to focus now on Dorkowitz and his geek.com computer club facing me from the bleachers. Our job for this part of the rally is to cheer and get the crowd rowdy when the players are announced. As if these boys could ever get worked up for a football game. They're bored by sports. The only net they're interested in takes a password, not a ball. What a letdown after being so high a few minutes ago.

Dorkowitz is blowing his nose, staring into space, or at us, who knows? They're all staring like that. I feel completely stupid now. The compu-wonks outnumber us, and I'm starting to feel like a zoo exhibit, standing there with my poms and phony cheer smile. It's ironic that I feel like a dork in front of them, instead of the other way around.

I'm standing in the "ready" position: feet are shoulder-width apart, elbows bent, hands pressing into my back, just above my rear. The whole squad is standing the same way. I'm panting a little, trying to catch my breath.

Maya is heading toward me, walking down from the middle bleacher aisle. She steps down and stops in front of me. "You were faboo, dah-ling." I keep my cheer smile in place and wink at her. We're not supposed to talk right now. She pretends she doesn't know that, saying, "Let me tell you one thing, okay? After the way he was checking you out, girlfriend, if you don't ask him, I'll tell him your middle name."

"You wouldn't dare," I hiss through my clenched smile. I simply cannot keep quiet after a threat like that.

"I swear I will." I stop grinning and give her my dirtiest look. "I swear I'll tell him your middle name and even spell it out, Peyton you-know-what Grady. So you better ask him."

7

I didn't ask him. But only because he didn't go to the game. I scanned the stands all night, hoping maybe he'd show up late, but he never did. I even thought maybe he'd swing by after the game, just to hang out in the parking lot with everyone like people usually do after games, but that didn't happen, either.

Hardly anyone was sticking around tonight. Maybe it's because we lost miserably. Palm Glades Prep creamed us, 28–3, and the guys were really down. All I know is that instead of catching my ride with Carmen, Lexie surprised me with an offer I couldn't refuse.

"Let me give you a ride, Prairie Girl," she said.

"I thought Beth Ann was riding with you." Beth Ann is a fixture in Lexie's passenger seat, almost like part of the car.

"She has to go home first. She forgot her sleepover stuff. Justin's driving her." So now I'm sitting in Beth Ann's sacred seat, in Lexie's red Jaguar convertible, hanging on to my door handle for dear life because she drives like a total maniac. The radio is so loud that my vital organs are pulsating.

She turns the music down a notch, yelling, "Peyton, from now on, I only want you to base for me, not Devin or Sloane."

"Why?" I yell back.

"Because you're the best. You're the strongest base on the squad, especially for full-on stunts."

"Really?"

"Straight up. You're the only base I trust." She turns the volume back up and ruffles my hair as if I were her kid sister. I'm overwhelmed. Here I am, sitting next to the prettiest, most popular girl at school, and she's telling me I'm the only one she trusts to hold her up. *I'm the only one.* Okay, granted, she's talking about trusting me during a cheerleading stunt, but still … that's pretty amazing. Especially for me.

Before I got into cheerleading, I was a nobody. Well, not exactly a nobody, but definitely a plain body. I felt like a grain of sand probably does. Just part of the mix. But being on varsity and getting to be with Lexie more and more makes me feel like a seashell, the kind people notice sparkling in the sand. Lexie makes me feel like I'm a somebody. She has that power. This must be what Beth Ann feels like all the time.

Beth Ann is so lucky to be her best friend. Maybe someday I could be like a Beth Ann to Lexie. Dare to dream.

Then high school would be the best years of my life, the way it's supposed to be, the way it is in *Seventeen* magazine.

Lexie races over the bridge that takes us onto Coconut Beach, the island where she lives. "Pay attention," my mother advised me this morning. "Tonight you'll see how the other half lives." I look out and try to catch every detail of the houses whizzing by us.

I've been to lots of houses belonging to Beachwood kids, and some of them are pretty fancy, but not like these. The mansions on Coconut Beach have marble stairs out front, security gates with guards, tennis courts, and pool houses that are twice the size of my apartment.

Most people at my school are rich, but not many are in Lexie's league. Maybe only the Garrets can compete with the Courts when it comes to money. Mr. and Mrs. Garret are in the newspaper all the time, blabbing about their philanthropy and posing with other rich people. Lexie's family is super rich, too, but she never talks about her parents, and they're not in the newspaper. I've known Lexie since she moved here from Manhattan in fourth grade, and I've only seen her mother a couple of times. I don't remember what she looks like. She's never even been to a game.

Not like my mother, standing in the bleachers, clicking away with her camera and shouting, "Look over here, Peyton, over here. Do a jump." I'm glad she comes, but the photography I could do without. When my dad's in town, he does the same thing.

As for Lexie's father, I've never, ever seen him and as

far as I know, nobody has. No one even knows what he does to have so much money, but rumor has it the Courts are worth millions.

Lexie turns her fuzzy steering wheel toward the iron gates of her estate, which open just in time for us to plow through them. She manages to slow down a little on the gravel road that goes around the side of her massive house, but it's not slow enough for me. At the exact second I'm sure we're going to crash into a wall that appears out of nowhere, she slams on the breaks. We stop only an inch or two away from it. I jerk forward and back, whiplash style, clutching my chest the way people do when they're having a heart attack.

Lexie snuffs out her cigarette, then pushes a remote clipped to the dashboard. The wall, which is really a door, slides upward, and we roll into a garage the size of an airplane hangar.

Four or five cars are lined up inside, but I don't have time to check them out because Lexie's already stepping into the house. I've been curious about her house for years. The Court mansion is legendary, and anyone who's been here is thoroughly questioned by everyone at school, including the teachers. I'm excited I'm finally going to see it. I'm also excited just to be alive after surviving the G-forces from Lexie's NASCAR driving, not to mention the life-threatening parking experience.

We're the first ones here. We go up a flight of circular marble stairs. Lexie skips some and I have to keep up with her, so I can barely take it all in. The biggest chandelier I've ever seen hangs above the stairs and the banister is cold when I touch it, made of silver, glittering wires. I follow her onto a landing and pass a library full of wood panels and wood floors, oriental carpets, and wall-to-wall books.

"Don't look at the parquet. It was our decorator's idea. We're changing it," Lexie says over her shoulder to me as I gawk all around me like a tourist.

We go through an archway and into a room that is basically a huge glass cube. Instead of walls, there are glass panels. All I see, from every angle, is the beach. The waves are amazing, especially because they're lit by a full moon tonight. I'm so wrapped up in the incredible view, I don't notice the two women sitting across from each other on leopard-print chairs until Lexie shouts, "Mother, what are you doing here? And what's *she* doing here?"

"Well, if it isn't little miss Susie cheerleader," says the woman. She's beautiful, another version of Lexie, but looks more like her sister than her mother. Her blonde hair is slicked back and her eyes are the color of a Special Dark bar, like Lexie's. And it's very obvious there's no bra underneath her white satin blouse. She and the other lady are holding wine glasses.

"What's she doing here?" Lexie repeats, glaring at her mother's friend. The friend has black Cleopatra hair and a slash of blood-red lipstick that matches her nails.

"I invited her for dinner," Mrs. Court answers, adjusting her strands of pearls.

"Oh, you did, did you?" Lexie's body suddenly goes stiff. Her eyes lock with her mother's. They're in a staring contest, with some kind of secret communication going on. I feel invisible. Lexie doesn't seem to remember I'm standing next to her.

Her mother cracks first. "Yes. I did." She sips her wine and gives her friend a Mona Lisa smile.

Lexie presses her lips together, breathing hard. "Has the Botox finally seeped into your brain, Mother? I told you the whole squad is sleeping over tonight." I should make some excuse to leave the room so they can argue without me here. I always get uncomfortable when people are rude to their parents.

But Mrs. Court doesn't seem to care. "You did? When?" She sloshes her wine around in her glass.

"They'll be here any minute. Did you even order the food?" The anger is building in Lexie's voice. I'm getting more and more uncomfortable.

"What food?"

"P.F. Chang's," Lexie says through clenched teeth. "I told you."

"So tell Lupe to call."

"Forget it. She won't know what to order." Lexie turns to me. "Stay here. I'll be right back."

Great. She's gone and now and I'm stuck with these two women. I don't know where Lexie learned all those manners she used on Mrs. Garret. I know she's mad, but she didn't even introduce me or say hello to her mother's friend.

Lexie's mother gestures to a leopard-print chair next to me. "Sit down, uh . . ." She raises her eyebrows, waiting for me to say something. I clear my throat, trying to figure out what she wants. Finally, she asks slowly, as if I'm mentally challenged, "What is your name?"

"Oh. Peyton."

"Sit down, Pane." Under more comfortable circumstances, I would correct her pronunciation. This time, however, it seems best to move on.

I sit. The chair feels furry. Then I realize, to my utter horror and shock, that the chair isn't just covered in a leopard-print fabric, it's covered in *real, genuine leopard skin.* I'm appalled. Wearing fur is so beyond wrong. Sitting on it is equally heinous. I'm disgusted and offended . . . but also fascinated.

Although I'm completely, 100 percent against exploiting animals, I have to pet this chair, just once, just to see what it feels like. I'm stroking its fur—scratching it, actually—when Mrs. Court asks, "Would you like some wine, Pane?" She sounds annoyed. Maybe I'm not supposed to pet the chair.

"Wine? Me?" Nobody's mother has ever offered me wine before. The only time I ever had wine was at Maya's bat mitzvah and I barfed all over one of the salsa dancers they'd hired for entertainment. He was spinning me around so fast I couldn't help it. I shudder, remembering. "No, thank you."

"Suit yourself," she slurs. She clinks glasses with her friend and they drink. I get it now. She must be drunk. This whole scene is weirding me out. There's a pair of elephant tusks standing in the corner and a zebra carpet on the floor. What is this, the carcass room?

I clear my throat again. A strange vibe is clearly in the air, but I guess I should still try to make conversation, being a guest. "I like your shoes, Mrs. Court. The rhinestones are really pretty."

"Thank you." She stifles a hiccup.

"Actually, they're Swarovski crystals, dear," the other lady says.

"They can put crystal on shoes?" I ask. I'm about to add that I thought crystal was only for glasses and chandeliers, when the Cleopatra lady laughs at my stupidity. It sounds like she's barking.

She manages to pull herself together enough to continue the shoe lesson for the village idiot, a.k.a. me. "They're Manolo Blahniks. From the Spring collection. I gave them to Bunny." She sips her wine and looks into Mrs. Court's eyes. Mrs. Court gazes right back, mesmerized. "I give lots of presents to Bunny," she adds, her voice dropping down a notch.

"You certainly do," Lexie's mother says. She slides a rope of pearls across her lower lip, and they lean in close to each other, whispering and sipping, off in their own world.

These two boozers seem to have forgotten I'm still in the room. Am I supposed to walk out or stay here, or what? I'm not sure what the sophisticated thing to do is, so I pet the chair again and watch the archway for any signs of Lexie.

No wonder her mother never comes to anything at school. Mrs. Court is highly bizarre. She and her vampire friend really give me the creeps. Maybe being fabulously wealthy makes a person forget to act normal around regular people. Just look at Paris Hilton.

I'm freaked out at this point. Where's the squad already? I wish I could just leave. I was looking forward to this sleepover so much, but right now I'd love nothing more than to be curled up on Maya's couch watching *Sixteen Candles*. What am I doing here?

Lexie comes back—Hallelujah, Amen—and snaps, "Let's go." She doesn't have to tell me twice. A quick "nice to meet you" and I can't get out of this glass taxidermy room fast enough.

Just as Lexie and I get to the marble staircase, I hear her mother's voice floating after us. "We should have sent that little bitch to Swiss finishing school years ago."

8

I'm still reeling from what Mrs. Court called her daughter. Who would believe that Lexie, Queen of Beachwood Prep, would have *that* for a mother? It makes me miss my own, a little. It wasn't a total lie when I told Maya my mom's been working late all week.

If I were Lexie, I wouldn't want people knowing that my drunken mother called me a bitch behind my back, so I've decided I won't breathe a word to anyone about what I saw and heard. Even though I want to. Badly. I mean, when you find out the one and only Lexie Court has a monster mom, you feel the need to talk about it. But I must resist. After all, there's gossip and then there's gossip.

Dishing about someone's boyfriend or best friend is one thing, but you just don't give out dirt on someone's mother. For example, I'm the only one outside of Maya's family who knows her mom got breast implants for Hanukkah. It will go with me to my grave.

I force myself not to think about Mrs. Court now, because the squad is finally here and I don't want to be a downer. The only one missing is Beth Ann, and of course Smellika. We're all wearing big T-shirts or pajamas, except for Sloane, who's in something very Victoria's Secret.

Everyone's on the floor eating Chinese food, watching MTV, talking, laughing. Even Lexie's joining in, smiling at something Devin is saying. It's weird how she doesn't seem upset at all, and I'm sure she overheard the bitch comment loud and clear, like I did.

"This was originally the ballroom, but I wanted it," Lexie told us when we all came up to her "room." It takes up the whole third floor of the house. "I can do whatever I want up here." She does a cartwheel to make her point. It's like a huge loft apartment with a cathedral ceiling. Everything, from the carpeting to the drapes, is pink.

I could never, in a million years, invite Lexie to my apartment. Forget that it's a shoebox compared to this. Between the old shower curtain in our bathroom and the cracks in our tile floor, I would die of embarrassment.

Lexie's talking about a ski trip to Aspen, inviting us all to stay at her house there. It's only a few doors down from Goldie Hawn's ranch. I would love to meet Kate Hudson. She's my idol. She's even flatter than me, but she was named one of *People* magazine's fifty most beautiful people.

The whole group is already making plans to go and

comparing travel dates, the best slopes and restaurants, the celebrities they've seen there. I don't speak Aspen. I've never been on skis in my life. I have no choice but to sit and eat my egg roll without taking part in the discussion. Instead, I'm busy figuring out how much money I can make if I work the Christmas rush at Bloomingdale's. They always hire extra help in December. It might be enough for the plane ticket.

Not one of them asks about the cost. It never ceases to amaze me how expenses don't enter their minds. Marisol and Carmen bounced in tonight with matching Michael Kors overnight bags slung over their shoulders. They probably cost as much as my mom's whole paycheck, maybe more. Worrying about money, wanting money, is just not part of their universe.

It's always in my universe. When these girls get brand new uniforms from Prep Boutique, I'm buying their hand-me-downs from the school PTO office for a dollar each. I see their names written in laundry marker on the tags. Just yesterday, I wore a Sloane cast-off blouse. If she only knew. It had a stain on the collar and my mom bleached it out. It would have cost thirty-five dollars new. I scan their carefree faces and realize they probably don't even know how much the uniform blouses cost.

I'm starting to be a downer again. Time to snap out of it and be social. "Hey, Sloane," I call out across the room. "What conditioner do you use? Your curls are so shiny they look almost fake."

"You really want to know how I get my hair like this?" It's so annoying when people ask if you "really want to know." If I didn't want to know, why would I ask?

"Yeah, tell us," Raquel says.

We wait for her great beauty secret. She takes her sweet time answering, crossing and uncrossing her legs. Sloane is the only one of us who's sitting in a chair and not on the floor. Finally, she says, "Lard."

"Lard?" I shriek, along with Carmen and Juretha.

Lexie cracks up, almost spitting out her soda. "You mean to tell me you actually put pig fat in your hair?"

"Sure," says Sloane, like it's the most normal thing in the world. "And then I wrap it in a shower cap and sleep in it."

"Poor Diego," says Shawntay, swallowing a mouthful of rice. "When you two move in together and he wakes up next to you wearing a shower cap full of lard, he'll think you lost your damn mind."

Devin holds a dripping piece of pork over the end of her ponytail and says, "I want to try it." Pinkie's high-speed giggles practically throw her into convulsions until she rolls around on the floor, clutching her stomach. I swear, the girl must have sucked in too much helium from her birthday balloons in pre-school.

"Ew, you are so gross," Lexie says, laughing. "Wipe that out of your hair."

Juretha waves a DVD above her head. "I TiVoed the cheer nationals on ESPN. We might get some ideas."

"Save it for later," Lexie says, shutting off the TV and sitting on a puffy pink velvet chair. "Time to plan Operation Smellika. If you're done eating, toss your plates. Kaitlyn, off my treadmill. Now. Can you grab me a soda from the mini-fridge? Thanks. And pass me that notebook, there, on the desk next to you. Let's make a list." Lexie loves lists. We gather around her on the floor. Devin and Raquel light up cigarettes.

"Beth Ann's not here yet," I point out.

Marisol says, "Yeah, where is she?"

Lexie checks her watch. "In Justin's pants by now, I'm sure. Or stuffing her face with doughnuts. Don't worry, we'll catch her up."

The jokes about Smellika start flying around the room. They're hilarious. I'm giddy from laughing so much. She's so easy to make fun of. I almost forget she's a real person. Devin does an imitation of Smellika's walk that sends everybody into full-blown hysterics and makes Pinkie run to the bathroom, holding her crotch like a toddler.

After a few minutes of ripping Smellika to shreds, we calm down and throw out hazing suggestions. I come up with the first one. "We could trip her, or maybe pull her backpack off and dump everything out." It's lame and nobody's really that excited about it, but Lexie mutters, "It's a start," and writes it down anyway. We work on the list for a half hour.

Operation Smellika

1. *Trip her. Dump her backpack.*

2. *Ambush her on the toilet and take a picture. Send it to everyone. Blow up hard copies and hang them all over the school.*

3. *Set up a Smellika is a Smelly Retard website and a page on MySpace, plus a group on Facebook. Do a fake blog pretending to be her.*

4. *Tape her ponytail to her head with electrical tape. Cut off pieces of her hair.*

5. *Break her glasses. Step on them.*

6. *Put an ant colony in her locker. Put dog turds in there too.*

7. *Put eyedrops in her lunch. Two drops causes the runs. Text everyone's cell phones with the safety alert that Smellika has a new strain of infectious Bird Flu and to stay a safe distance from her at all times.*

8. *Trash her car (key it, slash tires, etc.).*

9. *Crank emails. Write that we'll beat the shit out of her, that she's dead meat walking. Send her a cyber virus.*

10. *Steal her cell. Crank call teachers with it (pretend to be her). Call 1-900 phone sex operators.*

My stomach hurts by the end of our brainstorming session, and not from laughing. The hilarity stopped after number two. For me, anyway. Some people couldn't stop cracking up. They laughed more and more with each new suggestion, as if the thought of breaking her glasses or cyber-stalking her is the funniest thing ever. I know there's no way we can do all of these. Personally, I can't see myself doing any of them. Aren't some of them impossible to do without getting caught? And how do you fit an ant colony in a locker?

But everyone seems to believe we're going to go through with all of it. It's like they're in a frenzy. They've come down with Smellika fever, one by one. It's contagious.

Only I can't seem to catch it.

I wish we were all watching Juretha's DVD and goofing around right now, instead of writing out a set of instructions for destroying Ellika Garret. If she doesn't have a total breakdown, it'll be a miracle. This list is really depraved. And if we get caught, my life will be over: expulsion, no prom, a criminal record.

"Hey, Prairie Girl, you're so quiet." Lexie's eyes search my face. I must look terrified. "What do you think?"

I think this is serious and I'm petrified to go through with it or be associated with it in any way. "I don't know. I mean, I want Smellika gone as much as the next person, but..."

"But what?" Lexie interrupts in a cold, flat voice. Careful answer required here. I know she wants me to say the list is brilliant, that we should go for it and kick Smellika's ass, but I just can't. I don't think I have it in me to do those things to another person. "I'm just, um, not sure about some of it."

Lexie pulls her hair out of her ponytail, never taking

her eyes off me. She fluffs out the blonde layers fanning her face and asks, all slow and casual, "What is it you're not sure about?" My eyes dart around the room, hoping someone will help me out here. Sloane's eyebrows are bunched together. She's been pretty quiet too, like me. "Sloane, what do you think?" I ask. Everybody shifts their stares from me to Sloane, thank God.

She takes a deep breath, letting it out slowly. "Truth? I think we might get busted. Then we'll be up a creek. I mean, this isn't Mickey Mouse hazing. This is, like, full-throttle harassment."

Whew. At least I'm not the only one thinking clearly. It may be the most intelligent thing I've ever heard her say. Common sense has finally arrived. Now maybe Lexie will rethink everything.

"On the other hand," Sloane adds, "the alternative is that we do nothing and she stays on the squad, ruining every cheer, every routine. She'll turn us all into a total joke. I'd rather not cheer at all than have to cheer with Smellika." She shrugs. "I guess we have no choice but to go through with it."

Damn.

The words spill out of my mouth before I can stop them. "If we get caught, we could all be suspended or expelled. Or even arrested. I mean, what if campus security sees us slashing her tires or something? Do you guys really want to take that risk? For Smellika?" I'm nearly shouting. There's panic in my voice. It's beyond my control.

That gets everyone going. The room buzzes with worried voices. Lexie pulls out a box of Cartier cigarettes, lights one up, sits back, and waits. She takes a long drag, blows smoke toward the ceiling, then fixes her steely expression on each of us, slowly, one by one. The room goes silent. "None of that is going to happen." She leans forward toward me. "Peyton."

I say nothing.

"You need to lighten up and get on board with the rest of us." My insides shrink, hearing the ice in her voice push me away, so different from the way she spoke to me in the car. "Let's get one thing straight. If you're not with us, you're against us." She glares at me. "So, are you with us? Or not?"

It's not like I have an option. I nod.

"Good. Because if anybody has a problem with Operation Smellika, feel free to quit the squad. We only want team players here. You're sure you don't have a problem, Peyton?"

"No. No problem. I don't have a problem." She waits for me to say more, not convinced. "Lexie, I'm on board. Really, I am. I just..." *I just don't want to have to do the hideously mean things on your list, and I don't want to get in trouble.* That's what I want to say. What I do say is a vague statement like this: "I just don't want things to get, you know, out of control." My eyebrow is twitching. It happens when I'm really nervous.

"For chrissakes," Devin spits. "Chillax. This is no different from the stuff our mothers did with their sororities in college. Believe me, my mom's told me stories, and this is nothing." Some of the girls are nodding, like they can relate. My mother never went to college.

Lexie gets up and starts pacing. "Right. Hazing's a time-honored tradition, like senior pranks. And teachers always look the other way for senior pranks. It's their way of letting us blow off steam. Look, if we're caught pouring eyedrops in her lunch or itching powder down her undies or whatever, we'll just say it was a senior prank, not some big-ass deal. It's all how you spin it, you know?"

Naturally, no one reminds Lexie that some of us, including myself, are juniors. *That* could be a big-ass deal if she's counting on the senior prank excuse. And the stuff on our list goes way beyond pranks, no matter how you spin it.

"The most important thing," Lexie says, taking a moment to blow a smoke ring, "is that we do it when outsiders aren't around. Operation Smellika is our secret, and we're all in this together. If you guys keep your mouths shut and do it right, we won't get caught. Trust me."

"What if she tells?" Juretha asks.

"She won't," Sloane says, examining her manicure. "If she was the type to report us, she would have already."

Lexie nods. *"Exactement.* Besides, if she tells, we'll just deny it."

"But what if we go through all this and Smellika decides to stay, no matter what we do?" Pinkie asks in a tiny voice.

Devin answers before Lexie has a chance. *"Pffft,* like she'll stay. Are you high? I'd bet money she takes off after we get the snapshot of her peeing. We probably won't even get to do most of the stuff on the list." Devin sounds disappointed at the possibility. She offered most of the hazing ideas.

Lexie sits back down and drops her cigarette into a Hello Kitty ashtray. "Look, some of it sounds mean, I know," she says, going all soft and soothing on us. "But this is for the best, believe me. The truth is, we're doing her a favor. Are you seriously going to hang out with her? What, are you going to borrow her clothes?" A few girls snort over that one.

I can tell Lexie's just warming up for one of her pep talks, like she does before a game. She gets louder. "Are you going to double with her on dates? Come on, she's a beast. We'd do more harm if we kept her because every one of you would treat her like yesterday's garbage, anyway. You know it's true."

She waits for the murmurs of approval to finish. "Instead of prolonging her suffering, we're getting her to where she, and we, need to be. This way, Smellika and all of us can put this embarrassing episode behind us and move on with our lives. It's better that she be put back with her own kind."

Lexie has obviously mistaken Ellika Garret for a manatee, or some other endangered species that needs to be returned to its natural habitat. Juretha and Devin clap, they're so inspired by her words. Lexie makes Operation Smellika sound like a goodwill mission.

Since when did putting dog poop in someone's locker become humanitarian?

9

e's trying to crawl inside my mouth and rip my tonsils out with his tongue. My jaw hurts. I'm suffocating. But who cares? *I'm Making Out With Von Cohen!*

This is how it happened:

Lexie's phone rang right after her stirring manatee/Smellika speech.

"Hello," she answered. "Where have you been? Is Justin with you? Who else? Where'd you run into them? Okay, meet us out back, on the beach. I'll tell the guard to buzz you in." She hung up and announced, "The guys are coming."

The energy in Lexie's room changed right away. Everyone was instantly talking, grabbing makeup cases and brushes. If I'd known guys would be showing up, I would have brought my flat iron and padded bra.

"Which guys?" Marisol asked Lexie.

"Oh, you know, Hunter, Justin, the usual partiers from the team. And the skater guys, for some reason."

Did she say skater guys?

"Did you say skater guys?" Devin asked, reading my mind.

"Yeah, Justin and Beth Ann stopped at 7-Eleven for beer, and they were there. There's some skate park right next to 7-Eleven. Anyway, Beth Ann told them about the sleepover and now they're coming."

"Which skater guys?" I asked, finding it hard to breathe. Lexie didn't answer me. She just sat down at her pink vanity table and started applying bronzing powder with a makeup brush.

She was punishing me, sending me a message: *You shouldn't have said anything negative about Operation Smellika. Who do you think you are, questioning my plan? You should have kept your mouth shut.*

I wanted to walk away, but something made me stay in Lexie's force field. "Who's coming?" I sounded whiny and babyish. I knew I should stop talking to her back and leave, but I just couldn't. She finally turned around, and her coffee eyes roamed all over my face in this really intense way, like teachers do when they catch you passing notes or looking on someone's paper and they're not sure what to do with you.

"Please, tell me. Please." Why did I resort to begging? What was wrong with me?

I needed her to speak to me, that's what was wrong. I couldn't stand it when she ignored me.

She tossed her makeup brush down, satisfied now that I'd begged. "Whatzisface," she said in a bored way. "That guy the whole school knows you have a crush on." She snapped her fingers a few times. "Oh, yeah. Von Cohen." I flushed at the sound of it.

Marisol and Carmen overheard her, and they started whooping. "His hottie friends are coming too," Lexie added. "So brush your hair or something. You're looking a little sloppy." I felt like the tension was broken between us, a little. At least she'd answered me.

I didn't know what to be more stunned about: a) Von Cohen was going to be at Lexie's house any minute, or b) the whole school already knows I worship him. How did my innermost feelings become so public? Marisol and Carmen, most definitely.

Those two went crazy with excitement. They jumped over to me with all these teasing comments like, "He's coming for you, Peyton Grady," and "He wants you. He's going to be your luv-ah." Then they started chanting, "Go Peyton, go Peyton, go Peyton," and pretty soon almost everybody joined in.

My face turned as pink as Lexie's room.

~ ~ ~

I was amazed that Von knew exactly how to light up a bonfire. He said his dad's taken him all over the world on mountain climbing expeditions, and he's known how to make a fire since he was seven. What a man's man. He could probably survive on a desert island with nothing but a volleyball, like Tom Hanks in that movie *Cast Away*. Except Von's way better looking than Tom Hanks.

He and his two friends, A.J. and Mike, had taken the wood from one of the fireplaces inside the house. We all sat around the fire, drinking beers from a cooler and roasting the marshmallows that Lexie brought out from the kitchen.

Hunter and Justin were there, and two other football players, Stuart and Pete. Stuart seemed to be really interested in Devin, and Pete and Raquel were eating marshmallows from each other's mouths.

I always hear the gossip about who hooked up with who on the weekend, but I've almost never been at the parties where it happens. I've always been sitting on the bench, never in the game. Now I'll be the one on Monday who has the weekend scoop in class. This night will be the start of my high school social life.

Von sat right next to me, making funny, flirtatious comments. But The Great Moment arrived when he said, "Hey, you're shivering," and put his arm around my shoulders. His hand brushed my chest, but I'm sure it was an accident. I thought I would burst from pure happiness.

Having a guy put his arm around you is the best feeling. It's like he's saying, *She's mine. I picked her. She's the one I want.* And the icing on the cake is that all the popular people from school were there to see him do it.

Sloane asked Lexie if it was illegal to light a fire on the

beach. "Probably," she answered, shrugging. "But ask me if I care. If the patrol comes, I'll just tell them it's me."

"Hell, yeah," Hunter said. "You own this beach. Who do the cops think is paying their salary?"

"Exactement, mon amour," Lexie said, leaning down to kiss him. Lexie told us in the locker room today that Hunter loves it when she speaks French. She also taught us some dirty phrases in French in case some day we ever want to drive a man wild. It must work, because Hunter pulled her onto his lap and they started really going at it, full tongue, right in front of everybody. I'd only had a few sips of my beer (which, by the way, I think smells like the stuff they use to clean public bathrooms and it's beyond me why kids can't find other, nicer-smelling alcoholic alternatives) when Von took my hand and led me away down the beach. Somebody shouted, "You go, Peyton!" to my utter mortification.

And now, here we are, Von and I, lying against each other in the cold sand, kissing. He's as tall as me, and our legs and bare feet are all tangled up. The only other guy I really ever made out with was with a sophomore at cheer camp, and he wasn't that into it because he had a cold and couldn't breathe through his nose. I caught it two days later.

I never thought this day would come. I've imagined kissing him so many times that it's hard to believe it's really happening. He tastes like cigarettes and beer, but there's also a hint of mint, probably from the gum he was chewing earlier. I touch his tiny hoop earring with my thumb, while his mouth stretches out my jaw so wide I could swallow a truck and his tongue boldly goes where no guy has gone before. He smells like sweat, but in a good way, and some kind of hippie herb. It could be patchouli.

This is better then I imagined it. I have sand in my hair, but I couldn't care less. I want a sign-toting plane to fly over the beach with the announcement: *Peyton Grady is hooking up with Von Cohen*, so the whole world knows.

Breathing through my nose, remembering to keep my eyes closed, and trying not to get a stiff neck requires concentration. So I'm not exactly prepared when Von comes come up for air and asks, "So, Peyton cheerleader, are you going to ask me to Sadie's or what?"

He Wants To Go To Sadie's With Me!

I don't hesitate. "Will you go to Sadie's with me?"

"Nah, sorry, the Vonster's got plans that night," he jokes.

I toss sand at him. "Very funny." We start making out again. He needs to shave, and his stubble sandpapers my chin all numb and tingly.

I'm going to the dance with Von! I can't wait to tell Maya. I'll just tell her I asked him at the game. For that matter, I'll tell her that's where we made out, too. But what if somebody tells her I was here? Maybe I'll have to tell her my mom had to work after all, and this was a spontaneous sleepover, unplanned, an I-couldn't-say-no type of thing.

But she'll still be pissed. Whatever. I'll figure out what to say, but I can't wait to tell her about Von.

There's a piece of driftwood rubbing my thigh. I reach

down to push it out of the way, and when I touch it, Von groans. I stop kissing him and look down. It's not drift-wood.

It's Von.

And it's bulging out of his pants.

Omigod. What do I do with it? I don't know what to do with it. I'm afraid I might move it wrong. How, exactly, are you supposed to move your hand on a guy's driftwood?

Until I read the how-to manual, I'm not taking a chance on doing it wrong. I wrap my arms around his neck and start making out again. Maybe if I ignore it, it will go away.

Something cold is dripping on our heads. We stop kissing and look up. Beth Ann is standing over us pouring a few drops from her beer bottle. "Hey, love birds, come back to the fire. We're roasting marshmallows."

"Uh, *mucho* thanks, B.A., but we're kind of busy here," says Von. He plants his mouth on mine, and we pick up where we left off. She drips some more beer on us. A lot more. We both sit up, shaking the beer out of our hair like wet dogs.

"Come on," she says in this wheedling voice. "You guys can get busy later. Your friend A.J. just lit up a fresh one."

"Whoa, cowgirl, why didn't you say so?" Von says, perky all of a sudden. "I'm there." He's already standing, brushing the sand off his cargo shorts. I'm looking up at him and wondering what happened to our make-out session, decid-ing if I should be annoyed we were interrupted.

He pulls me up, squeezing my hand. "We'll finish this

later, okay?" I melt. I decide I'm not annoyed. I think I'm relieved. My jaw could use a rest, my chin is stripped raw, and we can't make out forever.

Plus, what does he mean by "finish"? I know that other stuff comes after the making out, and I have zero experience, as he could probably tell by my driftwood avoidance. Beth Ann might just be saving me from making a complete fool of myself. I wasn't even sure I was kissing him the right way. He could definitely tell I didn't know what I was doing.

Von and I hold hands walking back to the fire. We pick a spot next to A.J. and Mike. "Welcome back, Vonage," Mike says, making a fist and holding it out for Von to tap with his own fist.

I sit down with Von in front of the fire and try not to smile, but it doesn't work. Carmen, Marisol, and Juretha grin back at me, nudging each other and talking. I can't hear what they're saying because of the waves, the wind, and the flames crackling. Juretha leans over, handing me a skewer with a browned marshmallow on the end. The fire feels warm and good. I love the smell of burning wood.

A.J. passes Von a joint. Von inhales deeply and the scent of weed overtakes the wood-burning smell. He holds his breath and offers it to me, but I shake my head no and bite off a piece of my marshmallow.

"Dude, you don't partake in herbage?" He asks me. I love him calling me dude. Only a supremely cool guy could get away with calling a girl dude. "Try a J."

I shake my head no. I've never smoked pot. I've never even been near it. What if it makes me act crazy or barf or something? Von doesn't seem to care. He takes a deep drag on what's left and gives it back to A.J.

Lexie stands next to the fire, holding her skewer directly over it. She looks like a goddess in the moonlight in her long, white, clingy T-shirt. We can all see the silhouette of her shape. She's not shivering or rubbing her hands toward the fire like I would be without my sweatshirt on. I guess part of being perfect is that you don't get cold.

Lexie settles back into Hunter's lap. "We need to get Smellika off the squad. You promised you'd tell us about Cemetery Night."

10

"Ah, yes, good old Cemetery Night. It was invented to get this squid off the team back when we were in JV, our freshman year. The varsity guys set it all up. They picked Justin and me to do the honors."

"What was that squid's name, again?" asks Justin.

"It was, like, Howard or Harris or something," says Stuart.

"Yeah, I remember that Waldo," Von says. "I did roller hockey my frosh year and some dudes on the team wedgied him to his locker, wrote *fag* on his forehead, stuff like that. Locked him in the science closet."

We're all quiet for a few seconds, thinking about the science closet. The walk-in supply closet in the science lab is a holy terror to all of us. It's always locked, but no one will even sit near it. Besides housing dead frogs and worms preserved in formaldehyde, everyone knows the science closet also stores dead cats and monkeys.

That's bad enough, but the most talked-about specimens are the human body parts. Eyeballs, feet, ears, all floating in jars of slimy fluid. They say if you look on the top shelf, there's an actual deformed human baby floating in a jar of placenta. A real one. No one I know personally has ever seen it, but it's a school fact. I shudder, picturing myself being locked up in that chamber of horrors. Von puts his arm around me.

"He never narced on you guys?" asks Justin.

"Nah."

"He never narced on us either," says Hunter.

"So get back to Cemetery Night," Lexie says, poking Hunter in the ribs.

"Okay. You know that graveyard down the street from school?"

"Yeah, Mullins Cemetery," says Juretha. "That place looks like there should be a haunted house behind it. It's over a hundred years old or something."

"That's the one. We made up this long story about two axe murderers being buried there. Then we told him the whole JV team was going to sleep there, that it was an annual team ritual. A test of character." He swigs his beer. "What other lines did we feed him, Justin?"

"Uh, let's see, that it would bond the guys together, like a trust exercise, you know, a unity type of thing. Oh, and I remember this: it would give them the strength to face any situation. We copied that one straight out of my brother's frat handbook."

"Good stuff," Lexie says.

"Did the whole JV team sleep there?" Devin asks Hunter.

"Nah. We dropped him off at midnight and told him the rest of the guys were on their way. Then we left him there with his sleeping bag right next to the gravestones."

"Alone?" asks Pinkie, her eyes popping into two big O's.

"Not exactly," says Hunter. "I mean, he *thought* he was alone."

"But me and Hunter were there," says Justin with a laugh.

"What do you mean, you were there?" asks Pinkie.

"On the other side, behind some trees," says Hunter. "Getting our axes. Changing into our bloody jeans and work boots and squirting ketchup all over ourselves."

"Omigod!" I hear myself shout. "He thought you guys were the dead axe murderers!"

"You are correct, little lady," Justin announces in a game-show-host voice. "Hunter, tell her what she's won." Von squeezes and rubs my shoulder, meaning, *it's okay if he's being a sarcastic jerk and making you look stupid. I have my arm around you.*

"I hope it's a new car," I say, to show I'm a good sport. Not the best comeback, but whatever.

Lexie combs her fingers through Hunter's hair. *"C'est fantastique, mon amour."* To Beth Ann and Devin, she says,

"We could do our own version of Cemetery Night. But we'd have to do it ourselves. I wouldn't trust JV to do it."

"Definitely," Devin says, eyes gleaming. "So that kid, was he pissing his pants?"

"Oh, yeah," Hunter chuckles. "He flipped out. We totally punked him. He was all zipped up in his sleeping bag, eyes wide open. We waited before we came out, making these noises, rustling branches and stuff. And then we grunted and growled, or threw rocks. The kid jumped, every time. He must have wanted to bail, but he had no car, no cell phone, nothing."

"We were totally gory, too, dripping in ketchup, fake rotten teeth in our mouths," Justin says. "But that ketchup was too cold, man. Why'd you keep it in the fridge when we hadn't even opened it yet?"

"You did that, you idiot, not me."

Juretha asks, "How did you growl?" Hunter and Justin screw up their faces, grunting and gurgling. We all burst out laughing.

"Sounds like a couple of constipated bears," says Devin. More giggles.

"Then we ran out like psychos, yelling and swinging our axes," Hunter says. "We jumped on top of him in the sleeping bag and told him we were chopping him up."

"'Please, no, please don't kill me, please!'" Justin does a falsetto voice. "I don't know how he got home, but he took off running. Hunter, how'd he get home?"

"How should I know? The squid hauled ass out of there,

though, I can tell you that. He even left his sleeping bag. I was going to snag it but there was a big wet spot on it."

"Aw, poor thing," Sloane says. "You probably scarred him for life."

"Oh, come on, Sloane," says Lexie. "Who isn't scarred for life? We'll all be in therapy someday."

"Yeah," Hunter agrees. "Anyway, Cemetery Night worked. He transferred after that. Remember? I think he's at Palm Glades Prep now."

Lexie rubs her palms together. "Sounds like a plan. We need to add Cemetery Night to the list."

"We should film it," says Devin excitedly. "I bet we could get it on YouTube."

"What list?" Hunter asks Lexie.

"Nothing."

Von whispers in my ear, "What's the list?" I bite my lip. Lexie's watching me. Von's eyes are really glassy. He doesn't seem to be waiting for an answer. I don't say anything.

"Okay, baby, give it up," Justin says to Beth Ann, popping a marshmallow in her mouth. "Talk about the list."

"Give me that bag of marshmallows and maybe I'll tell you," Beth Ann says with her mouth full.

"Ho no, you will not," Lexie says, leveling Beth Ann with a sharp look. "Besides, you don't need any more marshmallows. Hello, your diet?"

"She can have all the marshmallows she wants," Justin says. He shoves another one in Beth Ann's mouth, but Beth Ann takes one glance at Lexie and pulls it out.

"I want to know about this list," Hunter says. "*We* divulged the great secret of Cemetery Night. *We're* trusting all of you not to narc on us. *We* trusted you, so now *you* girls have to trust us. It's only fair."

I don't know if she's had too many beers or what, but Lexie tells. When she can't remember some of it, we chime in and fill in the blanks. It's weird, but the list doesn't sound so horrifying this time around. She makes the boys swear not to tell.

They love the list. They even want to help. Mike's little sister has an ant colony he'll lend us to put in Smellika's locker. "She won't miss it," he says. He also says he'll put the ants in himself, if someone can get Smellika's locker combination.

"Dude, I'll do it with you," Von offers. He doesn't say much, but he does refer to Smellika as Sasquatch and Quasimodo a couple of times, and everyone cracks up.

Lexie walks around the fire and gives one of her passionate speeches. This one is about the power of togetherness. We're spellbound. I can tell Von is impressed. He's never heard her speak in front of a group.

She looks supernaturally beautiful walking around the fire in her see-through white tee with her blonde hair blowing around. "Now it's time to seal the pact. Operation Smellika doesn't leave our circle. We're sworn to secrecy. And if anyone violates the pact by telling or refusing to be a part of it, the rest will punish that traitor severely." We go around the circle and everyone says, "I swear on the pact."

I'm not sure A.J. and Mike know what they're swearing about because they're stoned out of their gourds, but they swear along with the rest of us. Lexie ends our pledge by saying, "Whatever happens in the future, remember the pact."

"Remember the pact," we echo.

It all seems like a dream. I'm so sleepy. I can barely keep my eyes open. Von looks like he's about to nod off, too. The fire's almost out, and Stuart and Pete are getting up, swinging their keys. Some of the girls start walking back toward the house.

Von and I hold hands all the way back to his car. He programs my phone number and email address into his Sidekick before driving off with A.J. and Mike. Then I walk back to the house as slowly as I can. I don't want this night to end, but I'm too tired to go on.

No one is on the beach anymore. I guess I'm the last to go in. There's so much to think about, but I know I'll fall into a mind-numbing sleep as soon as my head hits the pillow. My emotions have been on a roller coaster for the last seven hours, and I'm exhausted. This has been the most fun, the most incredible night I've ever had in my life. I don't know if any night will ever compare to it.

But you never know. Sadie's is coming up.

11

The phone is ringing, interrupting my nap. I only got a few hours of sleep at Lexie's. I kept waking up, thinking about Von, Lexie, the hazing list, everything. The minute I got home and saw my own bed, I crashed.

"Hello?" I yawn into the phone.

"I want my cell phone back."

"Maya, omigod. I have so much to tell you."

"I want my cell phone back. You still have it."

"Huh? Okay, but listen, you'll never believe—"

"Just give me my damn cell phone Monday morning."

"Maya, what's wrong?"

"Like you don't know." She hangs up on me, and I'm left with the dial tone humming in my ear. I call her right back. She answers after the first ring. "How was your mother-daughter night?" Click. Dial tone.

I sit straight up, my mind racing. She couldn't have

found out this fast. I punch in her number again. I don't know what to tell her, but I have to call her back. It rings and rings; then the greeting comes on. *Hi, this is Maya. Leave a message and I'll get back to you ASAP. Beeeep.*

"Maya, I know you're upset, but we need to talk about it. I can explain everything." I don't know how I'm going to explain, but I say it again anyway. "I can explain. Come on, Maya. Don't do this." I wait, but she doesn't pick up. "Please, pick up, Maya mooch. Please."

She picks up. "Explain away." I can picture her chewing the inside of her cheek like she does when she's angry. "Explain why you lied to me so you could ditch me for Lexie and your little cheerleader crew."

"I didn't ditch you for them." *I did ditch you for them. That's exactly what I did.*

"You did too, Peyton. You've been ditching me for them this whole week. Like when you wouldn't come over for dinner because of that dumb 'emergency' meeting."

"There was nothing I could do about that. It was mandatory."

"And practice after school."

"Mandatory. Look, just let me—"

"All I know is that I'm in Europe all summer, I can't wait to come home and see you, and it's like, I don't know, it's like you don't even care whether I'm around or not."

"I do care. Of course I want you around. You're my best friend." I thought about Maya all summer too. I thought about her every time I got a postcard from the Louvre or the Acropolis, while I slept on the floor of my dad's one-room apartment in New York, babysitting his actor friends' kids while they went on castings. Granted, it was fun shlepping them all over the city, feeling grown up and independent, but it's not exactly riding a gondola in Venice, is it?

Maya's still ranting. "I sent you a postcard every other day. I couldn't wait to see you when I got back, but all you care about is cheering. To the point where you make up some ridiculous lie to get out of sleeping over at my house, when you were just getting rid of me again for Lexie and her stupid sleepover."

"That was mandatory too. God, Maya, would you let me explain?"

Maya snorts. "No need. I get it. A sleepover's always mandatory."

"It was. It was a brainstorming session. See, Lexie emailed us about, well, about this problem we need to take care of, and—"

"Maybe I should have told you my sleepover was mandatory. Or maybe if I were a *cheerleader,* you would have come. That would make me worthy, right?"

"Can I talk? Please?"

"Go ahead. I'm dying to hear."

I take a deep breath, winding up to tell her why it was so important to go to the sleepover—some fictional version, since Operation Smellika has to be a secret—when I realize I have nothing to say. I just exhale heavily into the phone, feeling like a balloon that's just had the air popped out of it, all shriveled and empty inside.

I've never kept a big secret from Maya before. The sleepover was the first time I ever told her a stone-cold lie, and now I'm in so deep I don't know how to cover up anymore.

I can't think of anything to say.

The dead air on the phone is deafening. "I see," Maya says, her voice cracking. Now I can picture her nose getting red like it does just before she cries. It makes my throat choke up.

"I'm so sorry, Maya." It's all I can manage, before my own tears start.

"You should be," she sobs before hanging up, and the hurt in her voice kills me.

~ ~ ~

Mom knows Maya and I got into a fight because she "couldn't help but overhear." A likely story. I'm just glad she's not asking what the fight was about. She's probably waiting for me to tell, but I'm not going to. Mom's on a need-to-know basis about certain things, such as the fifty-eight on my trig quiz.

She decides I need some cheering up, so she cancels her hair appointment and takes me shopping. That is really motherly love, because her roots seriously need a touch-up. The black is showing, and I know how much she likes people to think she's a natural redhead. Props for Mom for throwing her two-toned hair into a bun and treating me to retail therapy. I'll have to remember this one.

We go to the Goodwill store in Palm Beach, near Worth Avenue. Mom's theory is that the closer a Goodwill is to the *uber*-wealthy set, the better the clothes. We find a great pair of Chip and Pepper low-rise jeans with beaded appliqués on the pockets. Fifteen bucks! I've seen them for around two hundred. They're too short, but with the cuffs rolled up, they make cute capris.

"Oh, they're perfect for the dance," Mom says. "They look gorgeous on you."

I'd told her about Von while we were in the car. She's beyond excited that I've finally made it onto a guy's radar. After I'd answered her millionth question about him, she pulled over and hugged me forever like I was leaving for Iraq, then grabbed my face and gave this really long sigh, like she's relieved or something.

Did she think no one would ever date me? Did she think her daughter was a hopeless case who would live out the rest of her days alone, with only cats for company? Did she think the words "Grady, party of one, your table is ready" were in my future? It's one thing when you have those doubts about yourself, but when you discover your mom may have them about you, it's highly disturbing.

I feel so bummed and guilty about Maya, I can't even bring myself to let Mom buy me the jeans. I have to punish myself. "I love them, Mom, but I can't get them."

"Whyever not?"

"Because everybody's wearing overalls, not jeans. It's Sadie Hawkins. It's a country theme." We discussed the overalls versus jeans issue in the locker room last week. Overalls won, but some girls on the squad are still wearing jeans.

"You are not wearing overalls, Missy. Overalls are for herding goats, not going to a dance with a boy." I don't argue. Mom should know. She grew up herding goats *and* wearing overalls.

I turn around and look back at myself in the floor-length mirror. Not too tight, not too loose. I look good. And I want to look good for Von.

"That is one fine bee-hind, Miss Grady," says a familiar voice behind me. "Yes, ma'am, you got a cute petoot. Now come gimme some sugar."

"Uncle Jeb, I didn't know you were coming," I say, smiling and happy for the first time since I woke up. I kiss him on the cheek and give him a bear hug.

"I wanted to surprise you," my mother says. More props for Mom. I adore Uncle Jeb. Mom leans over and kisses him. Well, kind of kisses him. They always do this cheek-to-cheek thing, but their lips only kiss air.

Uncle Jeb isn't really my uncle. He's my mother's best friend. He lived on the farm right next to my grandpa's farm in Byoots, West Virginia. Mom and Uncle Jeb have known each other since they were in diapers, and they both grew up with the same dream: getting out of Byoots.

On the last day of high school, they skipped graduation and escaped to New York together. Mom became a model, and Uncle Jeb went to college and became an engineer for Black and Decker. He designs vacuum cleaners. It's incredible that they both wound up in South Florida, with him in South Beach and us in Boca.

It would make a beautiful love story, except that, as my grandma puts it, "That Jeb's as queer as a three dollar bill, 'though by golly, you'd never know it." Grandma is so ignorant, she actually thinks that's a compliment. She means because he's not very fem. When Mom told Grandma that Uncle Jeb was gay, Grandma said, "But he can't be. He's not all swishy and girly-like." Mom says that people from Byoots are mushrooms: they grow in the dark. Scary.

Every time I see Uncle Jeb, we follow a script. I start it off now. "So, how's the vacuum business?"

"It sucks." We laugh on cue.

"Don't you think these jeans look hot on her?" Mom asks, her Appalachian accent going up a notch. She just said "own" instead of "on." They both talk more West Virginian when they get together.

"Oh, absolutely. Hotter than a snake in a frying pan. Love the appliqués."

"See?" Mom says. "Jeb thinks you should wear these to the dance."

"He didn't say that, Mom."

"Dance? Dance? Our Peyton is going to a dance? Don't tell me that. Lord, it makes me feel ancient. Oh, look at that old Madonna T-shirt." Uncle Jeb always gets ADD in any kind of store. "Remember my Madonna poster, Janie?"

He's the only one who calls Mom Janie. She changed her name to Jan when she got to New York.

"Yep, hanging right over your bed. You weren't fooling a soul with it, by the way. I reckon if you were straight, you would have had one of those cover girls, like Christy Brinkley."

"For your information, Madonna fooled my daddy for a long time." Uncle Jeb holds up a shirt to me. "So, do you have a date for this dance?"

"Yes," I answer, looking in the mirror again. I'm liking these jeans more and more.

"So what's his name, this stud who's taking you to the dance?" he asks.

"Von."

"Von what?"

"Cohen."

"His name is Von Cohen?" Uncle Jeb's laugh is just one long wheeze. It sounds like he's having an asthma attack, he's wheeze-laughing so hard. I fold my arms, waiting for him to finish. At last, he pulls himself together and asks, "What in the Sam Hill kind of a name is Von Cohen?" I ignore him, so he turns to my mother, "So have you taken a shine to this, uh, Von Cohen?"

"I've never had the pleasure of meeting him."

"Oh, a mystery man, hmm? And why doesn't Peyton want Von Cohen to see her in those sexified jeans?"

"Because most girls will be wearing overalls," I say.

"Overalls? Overalls? What are you going to accessorize

with, a pitchfork? Take it from me, honey, overalls are for baling hay and soaking up mud on the farm. If I never see another pair of god-awful overalls, I'll die a happy man."

"Amen," my mother says. They exchange knowing looks.

Uncle Jeb flips through hangers of halter tops while he talks. "Besides, you're not most girls. Be different. Give a rebel yell. Land sakes, what are you thinking, hiding that tiny waist of yours under big ol' baggy overalls. Here, try on this top."

"No, put it back. It's see-through," Mom says, yanking it out of Uncle Jeb's hand and hanging it back on the rack.

"Please, Mom. Only the bottom half is see-through. The top is lined. Everybody wears stuff like this." Mom is so conservative. Not me. Someday I plan to pierce my belly button and wear a dangling blue crystal belly ring.

"You just heard Uncle Jeb. You're not everybody."

"But Mom—"

"And I'm not everybody's mother. It looks cheap."

Uncle Jeb pulls the shirt back off the rack and holds it up to my face. It's a pretty shade of purple. "Come on, Janie, let her show off her Yankee shot. At her age, it's cute."

"Yeah, Mom, let me show my Yankee shot." I have no idea what a Yankee shot is.

"Nope, and that's final," says Mom, taking it out of his hand and hanging it back up with a loud *clink*.

"Oh, Janie, I wish you'd think outside the bun," says Uncle Jeb.

"See-through halter tops are low class," she says. My

mother divides all clothing and grooming into two categories: low class or classy. For example, belly shirts, tattoos, and acrylic nails are low class. Black pants, French manicures, and stud earrings are always classy. I'd like to know how she got to be such an authority on class, considering that the class system in Byoots was determined by whether you lived on a paved road.

I point this out to Uncle Jeb and he says, "Well, we lived on the only paved road for miles. I reckon that made us the king and queen in town."

"Which one of you was the queen?"

Big, long wheeze. "Good one, honey. Good one."

"Finding everything okay?" A hippie lady asks from behind the register.

I'm about to say yes when Uncle Jeb asks, "Do you happen to have that Madonna tee in a men's large?" My mother gives him an *are you crazy?* look. He answers it with, "What, it's for a friend. Fine. It's for me, for my 1985 collection. I love nostalgia. Is that so wrong?"

It's no shocker that they don't have a Madonna shirt in his size. He does find a great pink, chiffon, baby-doll top to go with my jeans, though, and a pair of Ferragamo black pumps for Mom. The shoes are only twenty dollars, a total steal. My mother only buys black because she says it's the only chic color for redheads. Again, I'm mystified as to what chic black attire she owned in Byoots.

When we go to pay for everything, the hippie lady says the shoes were mismarked and wants to charge more.

She must have heard us talking about the great price, and how Ferragamos normally go for hundreds. Uncle Jeb tells her that's no way for a charitable organization to do business, and it's an obvious lie, and furthermore, it's a crime they don't carry more Madonna shirts in men's sizes. He goes on and on, and by the time he's done with her, we get the shoes half off and an apology.

"You see, Peyton?" Uncle Jeb says, wagging his finger as we walk out of the store. "Sometimes you have to be a bitch to get what you want."

I think about that one. Do you really have to be a bitch to get what you want? I guess I'm sort of being a bitch to Maya, after lying and blowing her off so many times. Am I getting everything I want?

I'm getting a date with Von (my possible first boyfriend), membership in the Alphas, popularity, and a great social life ahead of me this year. It would be nice if I could get an A in trig, too, but for the most part, the answer is yes—it looks like I'm getting everything I've ever wanted.

Maybe it's true. Maybe I've always been too nice, and a person does have to be a bitch to get ahead.

It's just that I never thought I'd have to be bitchy to my best friend. She's family to me. I've always assumed Maya would be there, part of it all, coming along for the ride on my road to popularity. I never considered her not being around.

12

I've been rehearsing my apology to Maya all morning, all about how I'm going to be a better friend, how I'm going to make more time for her, how I'll never, ever lie to her again. This morning I got to school early and went straight to her locker. She wasn't there. I checked the *Beacon* office, the student lounge, and the breezeway. No Maya anywhere. So now I'm rushing to my locker because the first bell's about to go off.

And there he is. Von, leaning against my locker, backpack slung over one shoulder, sandy hair in his eyes, hands in his pockets. My stomach flip-flops. We smile at each other like we have a secret. I'm so glad my hair is smoothly flat-ironed this morning and my mascara has no clumps.

He leans toward me and gives me a quick kiss. "Sup? I've been waiting for you." His breath is minty. "Where were you hiding?"

"Nowhere," I breathe. "Just walking around." He kisses me again, longer this time. Just like he did on Saturday night, he stretches my jaw into a tunnel so his tongue can dart around in there. We stop, and I wipe the film of spit off my chin.

His mouth has a shiny, pink smudge from my lip gloss. I smear it away with my thumb. He smiles, surprised. I'm surprised at myself, too. Touching his lips is really intimate. It feels even more personal than kissing.

Something else flip-flops and flutters inside me, and it's not my stomach.

It's below my stomach, to be exact.

Von licks his lips, inviting me to touch them again, so I do. He kisses my index finger. The skin on my face is hot and prickly with this crazy, proud sensation. I never knew I could act this way with a boy.

It's like my alter-ego is taking over. The old, boring, boyfriend-less Peyton is dead, and the new, sizzling Peyton has finally arrived. I glance around, hoping someone is watching. I want people to catch the new Peyton in action.

Lexie, Beth Ann, Devin, and Sloane are hanging around the water fountain down the hall. Hunter and Justin are there, too, punching each other in the arm and laughing. I don't know for sure if they can all see me with Von, but I think they can, because Lexie keeps turning her head in my direction when she flicks her hair back, and I could swear she looks right at me for half a second every time.

She's doing it again. Now she's telling the others not

to look at me. I can read her lips. She's even turning her back, and they're all doing the same. A pang cuts me deep inside. Lexie's still hell-bent on sending me a message. Now she thinks I'm not a team player with Operation Smellika, even though I'm the one who stole the girl's uniform. I wish so badly that I'd kept my big fat mouth shut at the sleepover.

"Hey, over here," Von says, waving his hand in front of my face. "Dude, what's up with looking all over the place when I'm with you? I'm right here, you know what I'm saying?"

He's irritated. I have to remember never to look away when we're together. His green eyes remind me of two round bowls of pea soup. I want to tell him that, but he might not take it as a compliment.

"Sorry." I put my arms around his neck and kiss him a few times to show him I mean it. Also, to show Lexie and company the new me, because I'm sure they're sneaking peeks.

Yesterday's Peyton is over. Yesterday's Peyton would have been worried about getting a demerit for PDA in the halls. In fact, yesterday's Peyton wouldn't have even known how to kiss or what to do with her arms. Today's Peyton is sure of herself, sexy (okay, well maybe not quite sexy, but working on it), and totally secure with having a boyfriend, thank you very much. She's not afraid to touch his mouth and throw her arms around him and make out in the hallway.

"You forgetting about me already, Peyton cheerleader?"

He asks in a low voice that makes my eyelids heavy and my knees mushy.

Forget about you? How could you even suggest such a thing? I'm madly in love with you! I somehow remain extremely casual and jokey. "Yeah, who are you again? I forgot your name." Maybe Mr. Pappas is right about me having acting talent. If it wasn't for the occasional eyebrow twitch, you'd never know I was nervous. But only slightly nervous, because I'm the new Peyton, after all.

He smooths my hair back with the palm of his hand. My whole head tingles, even after he puts his hand back in his pocket. "Listen," he says, "I was thinking." He blinks a few times, like he's waking up. "Hyah, right. It's about Sadie's."

Oh, no. I knew it. This was all a huge mistake. He's going to tell me he was drunk, he didn't know what he was doing, he has a girlfriend, blah, blah, blah. Von's canceling on me. It's all over. I should never have looked away. That did it.

"Yeah?" I spin the lock on my locker, starting my combination. It will give me something to focus on if I have to stop myself from crying.

"'Scuse me, 'scuse me, 'scuse me," that high-pitched voice shrills, interrupting us.

Her timing is perfect, once again. She is the number-one most-annoying human in the universe. The last thing I need is Smellika breathing down my neck, witnessing my humiliation. I need to speak with Von alone so he can break my heart in private.

"'Scuse me." She's getting closer, heading straight for us. I think I could seriously strangle her for appearing at this crucial moment, if only I could see her neck. The problem is, she's being swallowed up by balloons. Only Smellika's tree trunk legs, the top of her sideways ponytail, and a few bits and pieces of her pinched face are showing. The rest of her is hidden behind a rainbow of balloons. She's a balloon tree.

I don't even want to know what her deal is right now. What Von is about to unload on me is more than I can handle. I'm sure it's all over. He's probably about to tell me our hook-up only happened because he was really stoned, and he can't go to Sadie's because he already has a girlfriend who surfs and skates and looks great in a bikini. What was I thinking, that I could get Von Cohen after one night of making out?

"So what were you saying?" I ask him as Balloon Creature arrives. I'm determined to ignore her and get his rejection over with. I won't even glance at her. I've learned my lesson about looking away.

"Get to class, people," calls Dr. Johnson. He's always patrolling the halls right before the bell, getting rid of the stragglers. His plaid bell-bottoms wave like upside-down flags as he marches by us. "And Happy Birthday, Miss Garret." He gives her a funny salute.

"Thanks, Dr. Johnson," she chirps. Then, before Von

can get a word in, Balloon Creature shrieks, "Can you believe this?" She steps between me and Von, invading our space. I have to move my head away so I don't get bopped by a balloon. Von looks at her like he's smelling rancid milk.

"I mean, can you believe this?" She asks again, tugging on a few balloons. What I can't believe is that my locker has to be right next to the worst plague ever to hit Beachwood High since Hurricane Wilma blew all of the hornet nests out of the Banyan trees and into our open cafeteria windows. At this moment, I truly do agree with Lexie. Smellika needs to *go away.*

Now she won't stop talking. I'm assuming she's talking to me and Von, but it's hard to tell since I can't see her face. "My mother surprised me with all these. I love balloons. They were tied to my new snorkeling gear. My parents are taking me to Atlantis, you know that resort in the Bahamas? And guess what, I get to swim with dolphins. How great is that?"

Von is staring at her like I did when I saw a one-eyed owl at the zoo. His jaw is just hanging open, like someone pushed a pause button on him. Apparently, Hurricane Smellika hasn't noticed that neither Von nor I have uttered one syllable to her, because she keeps on spewing. "Except now I don't know where to put them, 'cause there's no way they'll fit in my locker, and I can't carry them around with me all day, either. I mean, where am I supposed to put these?"

It takes all of two seconds for Von to squeeze my hand, say, "We'll talk later, dude," and disappear.

I rip open my locker, yank my books out, and slam the door shut as hard as I can. She flinches and that makes me want to slam it again, which I do, with gusto. Maybe she'll give me some space now. She doesn't even have the decency to be embarrassed about parading around with a bunch of balloons. If my mother gave me balloons for my birthday, I wouldn't carry them around if you paid me.

But Smellika, ever so perceptive, doesn't pick up on the kids snickering as they pass by. Lexie and the others are heading toward us, building up steam to make fun of her, no doubt. She also doesn't pick up on the murderous glances I'm giving her. She just keeps on going from where she left off, bouncing the balloons around like an eight-year-old. "I just don't know where I can put all these."

"Yeah, you only mentioned that, like, a hundred times," I mumble, clicking my combination lock shut.

"I know where you can put them," Lexie purrs from behind Smellika. Beth Ann, Devin, and Sloane pose on both sides of her. Hunter and Justin are gone.

13

"Yeah, bend over, Smellika" says Devin. "I'll shove those balloons up where they belong." We all laugh, even though it's not that funny. The bell rings, shrill and loud. A locker door closes shut and the few kids left in the hallway scatter. Our group doesn't move. I'll be late to AP English. I hope Mrs. Mandolini doesn't have a pop quiz on *Lord of the Flies*.

Lexie won't look at me. I'll prove to her that I'm all for Operation Smellika. "Yeah, bend over, Smellika," I say, trying to join in. Devin and Beth Ann grin, but Lexie doesn't even turn her head in my direction. She just stands there, snapping her gum.

Smellika gets very still. The balloons aren't bobbing around anymore. She must be holding her breath. Lexie blows a big bubble and smashes her wad of gum all over a balloon.

Bang.

I scream and grab my throat. Then I relax and laugh at myself. It's just one of Smellika's balloons popping. Everyone chuckles except Lexie. And Smellika, of course.

Beth Ann is holding a pin from her varsity jacket. She pops another balloon. Then another.

"Th-these are...for...my birthday..." Smellika's high-pitched voice trails away. *Pop. Pop.* Lexie jerks her head toward the rest of the balloons, signaling Beth Ann to keep going.

Pop. Pop. Pop.

Only three balloons left.

Then, in a move I don't think any of us expect, Lexie drops her backpack and yanks Smellika's ponytail, snapping her head back. With her other hand, Lexie snatches Smellika's glasses off and chucks them. All I see is a pair of orange glasses flying and balloons floating up to the ceiling.

Smellika screams. My eyes dart around, looking for Dr. Johnson or another teacher, a kid, somebody, anybody, but the halls are empty. We're alone. The classroom across from our row of lockers is empty. I never knew this section of the school is deserted in the morning.

But I have a hunch Lexie knew.

Smellika whimpers. A few drops of blood trickle down her pug nose. A nasty scratch from Lexie's nails. Smellika whines, "I'm legally blind. Gimme my glasses, please, please. You guys, please gimme my glasses."

I spot them near Devin, and they don't look broken.

I could easily point Smellika to where her glasses are. Any one of us could.

But we don't.

Smellika bends down, squinting and sweeping her palms all over the floor, trying to find them. She must really be blind because they're only a few feet away from her. Devin kicks the glasses farther away. They land near Sloane.

"Fetch," Devin says, like she's talking to a dog. "There's a good girl, fetch your glasses." My insides are weaving and churning. This is horrible. Smellika is completely bent over, crying and groping around on the floor. That's when Lexie walks behind her and kicks her in the rear end. Hard.

"Oomph," grunts Smellika, falling on her shoulder. She looks like a barrel that's been rolled onto its side.

Beth Ann sings out, "There's a good girl, fetch, fetch," just like Devin said it, and she gives Smellika a kick too, but it's only a small one, not that hard. Devin joins in and takes her turn, lightly tapping Smellika's butt with her foot, again and again, smiling like she does when we're performing a routine.

"Fetch. Come on, fetch those glasses, Smellika. You can do it, there's a good girl, yeah." Sloane kicks the glasses away when Smellika gets near them. Devin does too, twirling, turning it into a graceful dance step.

And Smellika crawls, feeling around for the orange glasses that are so close to her. Her scrunched-up face is all wet. Tears spill out of her eyes, which look so much smaller without her glasses. She's sniffing, making these squealing, snorting sounds just like the day Lexie pushed her down the stairs.

I don't know what to do. My back is pressed against my locker. I'm afraid to move. This whole scene feels surreal, like I'm a spectator at a horrific car accident. It's like I'm not really here, not really a part of it. Somehow we've all formed a circle around Smellika, and we're all watching this blind girl feel around for her glasses on her hands and knees. My eyes frantically dart around, half hoping we won't get caught, half hoping a teacher will walk by and put a stop to this. After all, I'm not the one who'll get in trouble. I haven't done anything. I've only been standing here.

Sloane keeps looking over her shoulder, checking to see if anybody's coming, but she doesn't look as scared as I feel. My shoulders and the tip of my head are trembling. Smellika's hand is right next to her glasses. She's about to grab them. Thank God. This will be over any second now.

But Devin isn't done having fun.

Smellika spreads her hand out, flat on the floor. Devin doesn't waste any time stepping on it. Smellika screams. I have to look away. My whole body stiffens. Someone will definitely hear and come to see what's happening. Smellika's screams are super loud.

Somebody's coming. Far away, down at the end of the hall, I can barely see her, a girl with long hair coming up the second staircase. Sloane sees her, too. My heart speeds up, pounding against my chest. Then I realize she's walking away from us.

You would think she'd come to see what all the commotion is about, but she's heading toward the exit on the other side of the building. Whoever she is, she must not want to get involved. Sloane shoots me a look that says: *Whew. We're safe.*

I watch the girl walk away, getting smaller and smaller, just to make sure she doesn't turn around. She doesn't. My heart slows down, but I still feel it knocking. She doesn't walk like a kid. Her walk reminds me of Coach Wisser.

But it can't be her. A teacher would be walking toward us to break it all up, not going the opposite way. It has to be a kid.

We all shush Smellika and Lexie tells her to shut up. She lets out a loud wail. It stops my breath, like a rope squeezing my neck. Devin keeps her foot on Smellika's hand and throws her other leg over Smellika's back, straddling her. She squats and yanks Smellika's ponytail, jerking her head back, then puts her other hand over Smellika's mouth. "Stop screaming, you stupid bitch," she hisses through clenched teeth, right into Smellika's ear. "Shut up, or I'll break every bone in your fat, piggy hand."

The screaming stops. Smellika pants and snuffles, trying to hold it in. She groans and winces. A green bubble of mucous escapes from one of her nostrils.

"Ew," Devin says, letting go of Smellika's mouth and checking her fingers to make sure no snot touched them.

"Please, please, stop," Smellika begs, sobbing.

"Maybe if you bark like a dog, I'll get off your hand," says Devin.

Lexie crosses her arms and stands over Smellika. She's grinding her jaw and chewing on her lip. Her eyebrows are scrunched together. "Do it," she orders Smellika. "Bark."

Smellika is in so much pain, she's pounding the floor with her free fist. "Woof." She winces and pushes out another barely audible "Woof."

I can't watch this anymore. My forehead is sweating. I might throw up any minute.

Devin grins at Lexie and Beth Ann before jerking on Smellika's hair again. "What? I didn't hear you, doggie," she says. "You'll have to bark a little louder."

Smellika is in agony. Two streams of tears run from each eye, dripping off her chin. Her nose has caked blood on it from the scratch. "Woof." Sob. "Woof." Sob.

Stopstopstopstop. Devin is satisfied. She lifts up her foot and says, "There's a good doggie. Now go fetch your glasses." But Smellika isn't feeling around for them anymore. She's holding her hand to her chest, whimpering.

Sloane kicks the glasses toward me. They land right next to my foot. Nausea surges through me.

Lexie pins her eyes on my face. They flick down to the glasses, then back to me. I check around again for teachers, kids, security, anyone. "Don't worry, Peyton," she says, ultra-calm. "It's Monday morning. They're all in a faculty meeting for specials."

It hits me now, how Lexie figured out we'd be all

alone. Smellika and I have lockers in the special electives wing. At Beachwood we only have specials after lunch.

Lexie must have found out that all the faculty who teach specials would be having their weekly staff meeting in the conference room. She always knows stuff like this because she works in the office for her community service class. She knows a lot of behind-the-scenes info about Beachwood.

Which explains why Lexie is so relaxed about hazing Smellika out in the open. There's no chance a teacher is anywhere near us right now, and all the kids, besides us, are in first period already.

Smellika is whimpering, still curled up in a ball. Lexie points her chin down at the glasses again, then raises her eyebrows at me. I look over at Sloane and Beth Ann. They stare back. Sloane nods at me.

This is a test. They're all waiting to see if I have it in me. Everyone else here has taken the plunge. This is my chance to prove to Lexie that I'm on her team, that I'm worthy of her friendship, that I'm one of them. *Give a rebel yell.*

I can do this. I have to do this. The new Peyton has arrived. *Sometimes you have to be a bitch to get what you want.*

I know what I have to do. I raise my foot, aiming it to come crashing down on Smellika's glasses. But something holds me back. My foot stops just above them, like it has a mind of its own, or some mystical force pulled the brakes on me. I glance over at Smellika's wet, puffy face. Her red eyes are unfocused, squinting into space. *She's legally blind. Stop. Don't.*

But it's the faces of Lexie, Beth Ann, and Sloane that get me to do it. I bring my foot down and stomp on the glasses with all my might. I grind my foot around, twisting up the frame.

When I step back, carefully shaking bits of glass off my sneaker, little shards are scattered on the floor. The frame is in pieces. I look at Lexie, expecting a nod or a "way to go, Prairie Girl."

But she's standing over Smellika, her chest heaving as if she's been running. Her face is purplish red and there's a line across her forehead. She's been biting her lips this whole time. They look swollen and strange.

It's the first time I've ever seen Lexie look almost unattractive. "Maybe your precious mommy should have given you contact lenses instead of all those balloons and a trip to Atlantis. Because now you won't even be able to see those cute little dolphins." Her voice sounds forced, like she's straining her throat. She bends down and picks up some broken pieces of glass, then drops them in front of Smellika's head. "Happy birthday."

In an eyeblink, her features relax and get soft again, as if she's waved a magic wand to change her face back to the one we know. It's amazing to watch Lexie flip her inner switch. She bends down and gently takes Smellika's elbow, helping her sit up. Smellika is sniveling, wiping her pug nose with her hand and gulping air in little spasms.

"Hey, Beth Ann," Lexie says, all sweetness and light. "I think she might need some help getting to the nurse's office." She pats Smellika's back. "That was a nasty fall, wasn't it?"

Smellika just sits there with her head hanging down, her shoulders shaking. "What fall? I think it's broken," she sobs, holding her own hand.

"Oh, bullshit," says Devin. "I didn't even put all my weight on it."

"YES, YOU DID!" she shrieks hysterically, startling us all.

Lexie brushes the hair out of Smellika's eyes. "It's time to calm down now, okay?" It's the tone of a preschool teacher soothing a three-year-old. "You know these initiation rituals are just part of being on the squad. You're the same status as JV as far as we're concerned. I don't give a rat's hairy ass what Dr. Johnson promised you. So if you want to cheer with us, you'll have to deal, just like JV. Just remember that. It's all part of our process and you'll just have to put up with it."

"Unless you want to quit the squad," says Sloane. "Then you won't have to put up with any of it." Lexie's eyes look cloudy. She gives him a blank stare. Did Lexie forget that the whole purpose of hazing Smellika is to get her off the squad?

"I can't do that," Smellika says, panic filling her face.

"Can't do what?" Sloane asks. "Quit the squad?"

"No. My parents...I can't. I can't quit, no matter what."

"Well, what a sucky coincidence," says Beth Ann. "Because we can't kick you off either." Lexie shoots her a murderous look. Beth Ann just shrugs. "She knows it already, Lex. Any moron would have figured that one out."

"Well, remember this," Lexie says, tapping Smellika's forehead with her index finger. "This never happened. Our initiation rituals are classified. Top secret. That means no running to Mommy or Daddy or the nurse with stories. The story is, you fell down. Got it?"

Smellika nods, still gulping in air, trying not to cry.

Lexie takes Smellika's chin in her hand and leans in so close to her face, they're practically nose to nose. "Because if you tell anyone, anyone at all, your ass will fry. Open your mouth to one person about any of our ... customs ... and you're dead. D-E-A-D. You'll be sorry you were ever born. I mean it. *Comprendez moi?*" She pulls on Smellika's hair again. "Now. How did you hurt your hand and get that scratch on your face?"

"I fell," Smellika says, as if hypnotized.

"There's a good girl. Beth Ann, take her to the nurse's office," Lexie orders. "I'm sure her mommy will want to come get her."

Beth Ann helps her up. They walk away in slow motion, with Smellika all hunched over like she has osteoporosis.

"Remember the pact," Lexie says to me, Devin, and Sloane.

"Remember the pact," we all answer. I look down the hall. Beth Ann is holding Smellika's elbow because Smellika can't see where she's going.

Because I broke her glasses.

14

In second period, Rude Office Lady pages the squad to the nurse's office. When I get there, most of the squad is there and Lexie is sitting on the edge of Smellika's cot, talking to Mrs. Garret. Smellika is lying on her side, facing the wall, with an ace bandage wrapped around her hand and a small band-aid on her nose.

"Did you give my regards to your mother?" Mrs. Garret asks Lexie.

"Oh, yes, of course," she answers. "She sends them back." She pats Mrs. Garret's arm as if they've known each other for ages. "So lovely of you to remember my mother." *Lovely.* That's what I mean about Lexie addressing adults as if she owns the business and they're her employees. Only Lexie could use the word *lovely* at our age and be taken seriously.

Marisol walks in with a birthday cake and sets it on a chair. "Oh good, the cake," Lexie says. "Surprise!" I'm definitely surprised. I'm surprised we're not in trouble. I'm surprised there's a cake I knew nothing about. I'm surprised everyone is acting so normal after what we did to this quiet girl lying here. Carmen and Marisol lock eyes, then glance at Lexie.

I suddenly remember a bunch of emails I skimmed over but didn't really read. Something about a cake prank.

We all sing "Happy Birthday" to Ellika. Mrs. Garret takes a bite and says, "MMMmmm, delicious." She takes another bite and says, "Mmm, Ellika, you must try this. You too, girls." We beg off, make excuses, say we just ate, that we'll have some later.

What Mrs. Garret doesn't know is that Marisol laced the cake with eyedrops (item #7 on our list), which have been proven, when used on JV last year, to cause uncontrollable diarrhea.

Mrs. Garret takes a picture of us with the slim, expensive-looking digital camera she just happens to keep in her purse at all times, in order to capture Kodak moments of her daughter. She also comments on what a sweet bunch of girls we are and isn't Ellika lucky to have made such nice new friends at Beachwood.

~ ~ ~

It's a miracle we didn't get caught. I wound up vomiting in the girls' room on the way to class, right after Beth Ann took Smellika to the nurse. Mrs. Mandolini didn't even bat an eye when I walked in twenty minutes late to English, all pale and shaky. I told her I was helping Lexie out in the front office for community service. Lexie gave us all fake passes stolen from the attendance desk.

Now it's lunch time, but I can't find Maya in the cafetorium. We always eat together at our own table. I doubt she's absent. She'd come to school in a coma to win the perfect attendance award again. I wish I could sit with Von, but he has lunch next session.

Eating by myself in public is totally out of the question. Even Dorkowitz has John Watson and Tim Ishikawa to sit with. Only Griffin eats solo because everybody knows he's psychotic and they're afraid to get near him. Rumor has it he once threw a chair at a teacher who was six months pregnant. I'll have to eat my bagel in front of my locker while I try to make sense of my trig diagrams.

Lexie and the Alphas are sitting at their center table, football guys on one end, cheerleaders on the other. I wave to Beth Ann because she's facing me, but I do it fast and keep walking, like I'm in a rush to get somewhere important. I don't want her to think I actually have no one to sit with. She leans forward and says something to Lexie, who turns around and motions for me to come to their table. Has Lexie decided to stop giving me the ice treatment now? I check my watch, as if I don't really have the time to stop and chat. Then I hurry over.

"And she just kept eating it and eating it," Lexie is saying. I'm standing behind her. She must know it, but she doesn't turn around.

Beth Ann adds, "Yeah, and she kept saying, 'Mmm, this

is delicious. Ellika, you should try this.' They've probably had the runs for hours." She giggles at the thought of it.

"At least Smellika will lose weight," Juretha says.

"Ew," says Beth Ann. "Can you imagine her in a bathing suit? Swimming with the dolphins?"

"Poor dolphins," says Devin. "She'll scare them. They'll mistake her for a whale." Everyone cracks up. "They'll see that jelly belly in a bikini and swim the other way." I laugh extra loud so Lexie will hear me. I even drown out Pinkie's Woody Woodpecker giggles.

It works. She turns around. Lexie's smile is a warm blanket I haven't felt in a while. "Need a ride home after practice, Prairie Girl?"

The last thing I need is for her to see my sorry apartment building or risk my life in her passenger seat again, but I'm so relieved she's letting me back into her sphere, so glad to be out of the cold, that I find myself gushing, "Yeah, thanks so much, I could totally use a ride."

"Where are you rushing off to right now?" she asks, then doesn't wait for an answer. "We saved you a seat. Sit down." She tosses her head to the empty chair casually, like it's nothing.

If I was invited to lunch at the White House, it would not be as epic as being invited to sit at this table.

To top it off, my seat is next to Beth Ann, diagonal from Lexie. A prime spot. They're both eating salads. All the girls are eating salads. I would have bought a salad too, if I'd known, even though I hate vegetables. "I have a meeting for the *Beacon*," I fib, sitting down. "I guess it can wait."

"What meeting? Am I supposed to be there?" Sloane asks. "I didn't know about any meeting."

"No, no, no. Don't worry about it," I scramble. "It's just a few people. Layout stuff. For my 'Last Look' article." I don't sound too convincing.

Sloane isn't listening anyway. "Do you know if Maya got my 'Shark Bites' column? I emailed it Saturday morning. It's really juicy this week. You and Von are going to be Beachwood's new 'it' couple after my column comes out."

So that's how Maya knew the truth. I can just see her reaction when she read Sloane's cheesy column. What a lousy way to find out. "Great," I say with a weak smile. "Thanks a lot, Sloane."

"You're welcome."

"What are you wearing to Sadie's?" Devin asks me, her face all rosy with fresh makeup. She's the picture of wholesome, like the girl on the raisin box. No one would ever imagine the hell she put Smellika through this morning.

"Jeans."

"Me too."

"Hey, Peyton," Shawntay calls from down the table. "You should let me French braid your hair for Sadie's. It'll look cute. I'm doing Raquel and Kaitlyn's too."

"Thanks," I say, trying to remember if Shawntay's ever said anything to me that's not cheer-related. So this is what they talk about in first-class seating. They're all acting as if I've always been sitting here, discussing hairstyles and clothes forever. But we all know the real deal. If Lexie hadn't invited me, I'd be back in coach.

The tag on my uniform polo is scratching the back of my neck. It's another dollar PTO cast-off, but I don't know whose. The tag keeps rubbing and rubbing, a grating reminder that while my shirt may look the same as theirs, it's not as good.

"Where's Maya?" Lexie asks me.

"I don't know," I answer truthfully.

"Told you she dropped her," Beth Ann says, as if I'm not here.

"Wait, I didn't drop her, okay? We're just in a little fight." That's all I need, a rumor to get back to Maya that I dropped her, whatever that means.

Marisol raises her eyebrows. "Little fight? That's not what she said in student council this morning."

"Why, what did she say?" I want to know. Maya doesn't usually talk about her business to other people, especially gossipy people like Marisol and Carmen. They're Sloane's best sources for her column. "And Maya was at student council? I thought she was absent."

Marisol's eyebrows shoot even higher. "Maya absent? Please. She's just avoiding you, girl. You should have told her about the squad sleepover instead of making up some crazy-ass story to get out of your plans with her." So Maya did tell all. How could she? We've always had an understanding that what goes on between us stays just between us.

"Yeah, that was a major blow-off," Carmen chimes in. "She's really pissed."

Lexie flips open a compact and checks her makeup. "That's what this gi-normous fight is about? How lame. Who doesn't make excuses to get out of a boring night? You can sleep over at her place any time. Besides, the sleepover was a squad event, and the squad has to come first." Sleepovers at Maya's aren't boring, exactly. They're just quiet. We watch a lot of movies.

"What's Maya's malfunction anyway?" Lexie goes on. "Don't get me wrong, I love her, she's great. But she's not really a barrel of laughs, either, you know what I'm saying?" Everyone's nodding around the table, agreeing. "I mean, who does Maya think she is, your mother? She needs to get over herself."

"Totally," agrees Beth Ann.

"Yeah, she really does," seconds Devin.

A sour taste is traveling up my throat and into my mouth. Hearing Maya criticized is like someone dissing my grandma or something. It's okay if I do it, but it's not okay if anyone else does it. "There's a little more to it," I mumble.

"Like what?" Carmen asks.

"Yeah, like what?" Marisol echoes.

I could tell them how Maya thinks I don't pay enough attention to her and all, but why get into it? It sounds dumb. They won't understand. They just want juicy details of our argument. But it sounds like Maya already told them all about it. She totally broke our trust. Lexie's right. Who does Maya think she is? Why am I being so loyal to her?

So I've been spending a little more time with the squad, so what? She *does* act like my mother half the time. I'm sick of it. "Did you know her mother got a boob job?"

Guilt swells inside me. I so shouldn't have said that. I so, so, so shouldn't have blurted that secret out, fight or no fight.

"Really?" Pinkie squeaks. "Mine too."

"Old news," says Lexie, snapping her compact shut. "I've seen her mother at our country club, positively popping out of her tennis dress, so obvious."

"So totally obvious," says Beth Ann. "Remember when her mom came to watch Maya in that debate last year in that low-cut shirt? And isn't Maya's dad a plastic surgeon? Hello, do the math."

Maya would die if she knew that everybody knew.

"Anyway," says Lexie, taking out a thimble-sized bottle of perfume from her purse. *Hypnotic Poison.* That's what it says on the bottle's tiny label. "You know what I think?" She dabs *Hypnotic Poison* behind her ears. "What I think is that you should try giving Maya some space. Maybe you've outgrown her, Prairie Girl."

15

I finally catch up to Maya in drama. That's where she was during lunch, hanging out with drama kids. As soon as I see her, the resentment I felt earlier melts away. It's true that she acts like my mother sometimes, but that's how she is with everybody. Maybe I could talk to her about it. I don't know why she told people about our fight, but I'm willing to forgive her if she'll forgive me. And I'll never, ever tell her that people know about her mom. It's supposed to be a secret.

We're backstage, lifting long wooden boards from a stack and spreading them out on the floor. We're supposed to paint them as backdrops for *Julius Caesar*. "I think Von might be more than a BOM," I say, passing her another board. She's pretending I don't exist. "Like a boyfriend. Although I'm worried he's already dumping me." I search her face for some trace of a reaction. I get nothing. "So, what do you think of him?"

Her face is hard and blank, just like these boards. "Come on, Maya mooch, you can't keep this up. We have to talk." Maya's always been so stubborn.

I hand her another board. "Maya, I messed up, okay? I'm sorry. I'm really going to be a better friend now." That twinge of guilt surfaces again. I wasn't much of a friend at the Alpha table. "Seriously. Let me make it up to you."

I'm about to explain how we can have an amazing sleepover this Friday, with all our favorite chick flicks, when Dr. Giles' humongo frame floats up to us in her long tie-dyed tunic. "Enough talking, you two," she says, which just shows you how teachers don't know what's going on in class, because only one of us is talking. "Paint these to look like columns," she orders before floating away, a billowing, tie-dyed tent with feet.

I was afraid Dr. Giles was going to beat me up when I came in late. She looked at me the way I look at a mosquito when it lands on my arm, right before I'm about to swat it. When I handed her my transfer slip, all she said was, "I'm not used to having an athlete of your stature in my class." I still don't know if she was making fun of my height or my being a cheerleader. I don't see how this is going to be an easy A.

Thump. Thump. Maya keeps dropping the boards I hand her and grabbing the next ones. *Thump.* Griffin and Compular walk past us carrying paint cans. Compular is whistling the theme from *The Simpsons.* Griffin looks ready to strangle him. Those two go together like chocolate and meatloaf. I can't figure out what either one of them is doing in this class.

Compular calls out, "What's up, Peyton? Don't forget, tomorrow, sixth period, tutoring." I press my lips together and sort of smile back. He goes back to whistling. I pray no one sees him tutoring me. If Carmen or Marisol catch me with him, the rumors will spread like a rash.

Thump. I've had it with Maya ignoring me. I reach inside my backpack and rummage around until I find her cell phone, then stomp past her to open the heavy, metal door that opens to a ramp leading down into a parking lot. I open it and raise my arm as if I'm going to chuck her cell phone.

That gets her attention. Maya runs toward me. I step outside. She follows, stretching upward, trying to grab the phone out of my hand. I hold it high over her head. She hates that. I've been doing that to her since we were five. The door slams shut. We're at the top of a ramp leading down into a parking lot. I don't know if we can get back inside. And I don't care.

She crosses her arms. "Give. Me. My. Phone."

"So, it speaks." I fold my arms back at her, gripping the phone. "Listen, Maya—"

"Peyton—"

"Just listen. I shouldn't have lied to you. I've been thinking about it a lot, and I know I haven't been a good friend lately, but that's all over now. I promise I'm going to change."

"No, you're not, Peyton. You care too much about all of it to change now."

"What do you mean, *all of it?*"

"Lexie's clique, the cheering." She rolls her eyes. "All of it. You think being a cheerleader is more important than life itself."

"More important than life itself? Wow, you're in the right class. Aren't you being a little dramatic?"

"Am I? Let's see. You don't care about me, your grades, or your SATs. You didn't even sign up for the prep course, and I thought we were taking it together. I mean, have you even given *any* thought to your future, what you want to major in? Where you even want to apply? No. You haven't. Because all you care about is cheering and hanging out with your new varsity-jock friends."

I feel an angry heat brewing. Partly because she's got some nerve, and partly because she's got some truth. "Exactly who do you think you are, my mother? You need to get over yourself, you know. Like, what's your malfunction?"

"What?" She scratches her head, confused. It sounded better when Lexie said it.

"Besides, the sleepover was a squad event and the squad has to come first sometimes."

"*The squad* comes first all the time! That's my *malfunction*, Peyton."

"Oh, yeah?"

135

"Yeah."

"Well, too bad!" I scream. "I've worked hard to get on varsity and I'm sorry you don't *approve*. Maybe it's just because cheering's the one thing you can't do."

"I could too, Peyton, and you know it."

"So why don't you?"

"Because I think it's stupid. I never tried out because I choose to use my brain, unlike you. Why is cheering so damn important? What does it do for you?"

I actually laugh out loud. Where do I start? "Well, for one thing, Von wouldn't give me the time of day if I wasn't on the squad."

"You actually think he wouldn't be into you if you weren't jumping up and down in a tiny skirt?"

"No, he wouldn't. It makes me stand out. It makes me special around here."

"You think the only way to be special is by shaking your ass and your pom-poms around?"

"Yes."

"To who?"

"To the whole school!" I shout, because it's so obvious and she refuses to see it. "Don't you remember the first thing Von ever said to me? 'Hey, aren't you a cheerleader?' That's what he said. Not, hey, aren't you a staffer for the *Beacon*. He said cheerleader. *Cheerleader*." I sit down on the ramp. "It matters."

"That's such a load, Peyton. Why don't you admit it? You just want to be in the same league with Lexie and Beth

Ann. Why do you idolize them so much? Is it the money, or what?"

Interesting how one question can make the only wall that's ever been between Maya and me come crumbling down. Make that one word: *money*. I'm numb. It's as if she's slapped me. Hard. "Screw you, Maya," I whisper.

How dare she judge me? She doesn't need to be in the Alphas. She's accepted by everyone. She's got a perfect body, an incredible wardrobe, a car to die for, and a top GPA. She has *everything* and it's all been handed to her from birth: a nuclear family—dysfunctional yes, but that makes it even more perfect because a non-dysfunctional family would be too Stepford—wealth, looks, and all-around popularity.

Why should I have to apologize for wanting more? She doesn't know what it's like to have to work hard at *everything:* having money, passing trig, being pretty, finding a boyfriend, having nice clothes, and yes, being popular. No one knows how much I *need* to be a cheerleader, least of all Maya Kaplan.

"You wouldn't understand. That's why I lied to you."

"Oh, come off it, Peyton. You've always had a chip on your shoulder about money. Poor, poor, Peyton. If I even utter the word 'scholarship' you practically have a convulsion. Can I help it if my dad makes a lot of money? You've always held that against me. I'm so damn sick of it."

"Because you don't realize how many doors that opens for you."

"Gee, thanks a lot. I guess money's always been my free ticket, huh? I don't have to work hard for anything. My extracurriculars, my awards, my GPA—it's all just bought and paid for with Daddy's money."

"That's not what I'm saying. You don't get it. You're... you're..."

"What?"

"You're not in the same position as me. Everyone likes you."

"Just because I have money? No one likes me for me? What, like money is the only thing that counts?"

"No, but it counts more than you want to admit."

"No. It counts less than you think. Besides, what can I do? I can't change things. I can't switch places with you. I can't run away from myself any more than you can."

"That's not true—you can change yourself. People reinvent themselves all the time. Look at Ashley Simpson." She manages a smile, just a little one. "Maybe you'd understand if you joined a sports team."

"My shrink says team sports undermine an individual's potential, and I agree with him. Actually, I should thank you."

"Why?"

"Because now I have something to tell him for our session this afternoon."

"And what are you going to tell him?"

"That my friendship with you is over." Hearing her say that makes me wince the way I do when I hear the crash of a plate breaking in a restaurant, or a loud crack of thunder on a sunny day. It's unexpected. Shocking.

Our friendship is over.

"I always knew you were a climber, but I never thought you'd step over me to get to the top," Maya says softly. "So go, Peyton. You've been pulling away from me since the summer. You're one of them now. Go swim with the sharks. It's what you want." Neither one of us is crying or yelling, neither one of us is devastated. She takes the cell phone out of my hand, stands up, pulls open the metal door and goes inside.

I stay on the ramp, hugging my knees. I wait for tears, but none come. I should feel more upset than this. It's strange that I don't feel anything—nothing at all. Even the little birds perched on the roof seem to be glaring down their beaks at me, as if to say, *What's wrong with you? You just lost your best friend. Cry or something.*

I inhale deeply, willing tears, anger, hurt, any feelings to come and get me. They don't. I feel curiously normal. How weird, after all these years with her. I guess we both knew this was coming. Maya's right. It's just over.

I think Lexie is right too, about me outgrowing Maya. But the real sucker punch here, the one I never saw coming, is that Maya's outgrown me, too.

16

"The functions of an angle are related to the ratios of the sides of a right triangle. See?"

I nod, pretending I get it. I can't tell Compular that he could repeat this nine hundred times and I still won't get it. We're sitting at an empty table in the music wing, near Dr. Giles' theater. It's a big, all-purpose room cut in half by one of those plastic accordion dividers. The flute players from our marching band are taking a lesson on the other side. It was my idea to come here instead of the library. None of the Alphas would be caught dead around here.

"Now, check this out. An acute triangle can be separated into two right angles if you draw a line segment from one of the vertices, perpendicular to the side opposite the vertex. Just like that. See?" He says this like he's just shown me the secret to growing money on trees, like it's the most amazing thing in the world. I've never seen someone so crazy about math. "See?"

I don't see. I'm too distracted by my personal life. I haven't seen Von, my ex-almost-boyfriend, since yesterday morning. Images of Maya's hurt face, Von walking away from my locker, and Smellika curled up on the floor are all swimming around and around in my head. It's impossible to concentrate. And the flutes don't help, which, by the way, sound more like starving birds in a feeding frenzy than musical instruments. I wonder how many music teachers go postal with nervous breakdowns after having to listen to this every day.

"What's up?" he asks me. "You're zoning."

"Sorry. I'm having trouble paying attention."

"Are you ADD?"

"No. I just have a lot on my mind."

"Have you tried amatta?"

"What's amatta?"

"Nothing, what's amatta with you?" He waits for a laugh, then mimes a drummer and says, "badumpump."

I roll my eyes. "That's got to be the worst joke in the world."

"It is, isn't it? But enough comedy. Let's get back to work."

I try to focus on Compular's diagrams. I *have* to learn this. If I don't pass trig, I'll lose my scholarship, and then I'll have to leave Beachwood. The thought of it drops a small bomb in the pit of my gut.

"And now, ladies and gentlemen, I'd like to present the law of sines." He cups his hands over his mouth and breathes out, making a sound like applause. I have to give him credit. He may be corny, but at least he's trying to make this semi-interesting. I stare hard at his diagrams, willing them to make some sense, but it's no use. So I just keep repeating whatever he's saying and copying his notes.

"Sometimes there's no solution when you use the law of sines," he says.

"Sometimes there's no solution when—wait a minute." I stop writing. "What do you mean, 'there's no solution'?"

"Not all angles and side lengths measure out to triangles."

"You mean I could work on a problem with no answer?"

"Well, potentially, yeah."

I throw down my pencil. "Oh, this is such a waste of time. I should be working on my F. Scott Fitzgerald paper now. It's due tomorrow and my rough draft is only half done. I'll be up until midnight working on it." I close my notebook.

"What are you doing?" he asks. "We still have twenty minutes."

"Okay, no offense, but I can't take it anymore. When in my life will I ever need to know the law of sines?"

"For your quiz on Friday?"

"And then what? I'm not going to be a mathematician."

"Quiet over there, please," Mrs. Kipfer, the music

teacher, calls out from the other side of the accordion divider. I didn't realize I was shouting.

"Sorry," I call back. Then I continue my point a little more quietly. "Anyway, when will I use trig in real life?" I close his notebook, making it clear that we're done with this torture for today.

He leans back, folds his hands behind his curly head. "When you're playing pool, of course."

"I prefer air hockey."

"We have two pool tables at our house. They're at the bottom of our pool. In the deep end."

"Underwater?"

"Yup."

I know he's lying, but I want to hear more. "Why would you do that?"

"Guess."

"Because you're nuts?"

"That, and ..." He waits, like I'm supposed to guess again. I don't. Finally, he says, "It's pool inside a pool. Get it?"

"No. How do you play?"

"That's the best part. My dad and I put on full scuba gear and play games down there."

"I assume you have oxygen tanks." I feel myself grinning. His BS is way more entertaining than trig.

"Of course."

"So, why do you have two pool tables down there? Why not just put one?"

"Because I'm building robots that'll play at the other table. Then we'll have tournaments, you know, man versus machine."

They don't call him Compular for nothing. "Who'll win?"

"The robots, if I program them right."

"Sounds very sci-fi."

"Nah, not really. Just high tech. So, if you're not going to be a mathematician, what are you planning to study?"

"I don't know. Maybe dance." I usually don't tell people that. It sounds too hopeless, like when F. Scott Fitzgerald's cuckoo wife tells everyone she wants to be a ballerina. I don't know why I just told him.

"You're a really good dancer. You were great at the pep rally last week."

"Thanks."

"Too bad Ellika Garret can't dance. She's so weird. It's sad."

I avoid his eyes. "I know."

"There's a text message going around that she's got that deadly Bird Flu."

"I don't know who sent that." It was Lexie. "But I know it's not true."

"Of course it's not true. Duh, if she had Bird Flu, she'd be under quarantine. The CDC would be involved." He snorts. "People are so gullible. They're treating her like she has leprosy. No one would go within ten feet of her in the halls when we changed classes." The flutes suddenly whine one long, irritating note all together.

"Good, good," Mrs. Kipfer says from behind the screen. "Now, keep your fingers on the B hole."

"Put your finger on your A hole!" Griffin yells, stomping past the door. He's heading toward the theater. The flutes stop.

"What's Griffin doing taking drama?" I ask.

"Yeah, I thought it was bizarre too, at first. He's choreographing the stabbing scene for *Julius Caesar*. He's really serious about it."

"Yeah, but come on, drama? Shouldn't he be in metal shop, sharpening his knives or making bullets? I mean, why does a future serial killer register for drama?"

"Don't joke. He'll slaughter me if I tell you."

"You actually talked to him?" I'm amazed. Nobody talks to Griffin. The only exchange I've ever had with him was in eighth grade PE when I struck out with all the bases loaded and he asked if I was born a "friggin' spaz" or did I work on it and I mumbled back an apology. "What did he say? Why is he in drama?"

"I can't tell you."

"Please. You have to. Promise I won't tell."

"You better not, or my murder will be on your conscience."

"Just tell me already."

"He wants to be a wrestler. He thinks drama will help him with his character."

"What character?"

"The Boca Boulder." I blink at him. "You know, like that wrestler, The Rock? Get it? Rock...boulder..."

My laughter escapes in great big bubbles of sound. The mental picture of Griffin wearing a cape and tights is so funny, I'm rocked by wave after wave of giggles. Compular can't help but join in. His dimples form deep lines in his cheeks. I keep sputtering, "the Boca Boulder," laughing until my sides hurt. I'm gasping for air when I look up and see Von's golden hair at the door.

"What's so funny?" Von asks, coming into the room. Compular and I manage to calm down pretty quickly. "Yo, what's the joke?"

I clear my throat. "Oh, it's nothing." I glance at Compular, who's staring at the band-aid on Von's ear, the one that hides his earring. Von notices, and rubs it self-consciously before leaning down to give me a quick kiss on the mouth.

Even though we made out in the hallway yesterday, I'm embarrassed he just kissed me in front of Compular. It just seems weird and awkward to kiss right now, in the middle of tutoring, with one person watching. Von and Compular say "hey" to each other, then nobody says anything for a few seconds. Compular examines his hands. I'm highly uncomfortable.

"What are you doing here?" I ask Von.

"Finding you. What are *you* doing here?"

"Oh, just a little tutoring."

"Could I talk to you for a minute?" He tosses his head toward the door. "In my private office?"

"Sure," I say, jumping up so fast I knock my notebook onto the floor. I pick it up and say, "Be right back" to Compular, then follow Von into the hallway.

"The librarian told me you were here," he says, leaning against the wall.

"Oh." *Just go ahead and dump me. I'm ready.* "Didn't you want to tell me something about Sadie's?"

"Yeah, I just wanted to ask you something. I was, uh, wondering if you want to come see me jam with my band after."

"What?"

"Yeah, I play drums in this band, and we sorta have a gig the same night at Club Hole, but, like, I'm stoked to go to the dance with you, too. So I was kinda hoping we could do both. Like hit the dance first and then my gig." He takes a deep breath and exhales through his full lips. "But only if that's cool with you. If you're not into it, no worries."

If that's cool with me? Not only does he still want to go to Sadie's and isn't breaking up with me, but he also wants to take me to a rock club. He used the word "stoked" about going to the dance with me! Oh, why did I ever doubt you, Von?

"Omigod, yes," I gush. "I would *love* to see you play with your band."

"Cool." He looks relieved, which is so ironic, because I'm the one who's over-the-top relieved. "Gotta get back to class," he says, and gives me a mouth-stretching kiss. I can see him now, all sexy, drumming. Possibly with his shirt off.

That flutter just came back.

17

Dr. Giles wants us to write in a journal for a week. It's supposed to be private. The idea is for us to look back and read how we were feeling on a particular day so we can recall that emotion for our acting. We're supposed to observe people and things in our daily life and write about them. I don't see why I have to do this if I'm only on stage crew, but here we go:

THURSDAY, SEPTEMBER 16

Operation Smellika is in full swing. The *Smellika is a Smelly Retard* website is fully operational, along with the Smellika MySpace page and Facebook group. Word is spreading all over school. Justin and Hunter set it all up.

When you open the website, there's the snapshot that Marisol and Carmen took, of Smellika sitting on the toilet. Her mouth is open wide like she's sucking in air, and her skort is around her ankles. They hid in the bathroom and ambushed her right after lunch, like paparazzi. After the picture, there's a poll to vote on Smellika's ugliest feature.

By the way, Smellika has new glasses now. They're colorless instead of orange, and they're still an inch thick, but they look halfway normal.

Friday, September 17.

We saw the top half of Smellika's naked butt in Pavlich's class today. Beth Ann was sitting behind Smellika with a pair of cuticle scissors, and when Smellika leaned forward to write, Beth Ann cut the back of her skort. Lexie loved it and told her to keep going. So Beth Ann kept cutting from the waistband down, and Smellika didn't feel anything!

Her underwear and some of her crack were showing. The whole back row was leaning over to see, muffling laughs. Pavlich croaked, "What are you all looking at, boys and girls?" and Justin goes, "Just the surface of the moon, Mrs. Pavlich."

Then Smellika turned around and realized she had a bad case of plumber butt. She jumped up and moaned, "oh, no," and ran out of the room holding the back of her skort with her hands. Mrs. Pavlich was all confused and asked, "Why did she leave?" and then Justin goes, "Maybe she's em-*bare-assed*."

My stomach started doing that knot thing again and it must have showed on my face because Lexie goes, "Peyton, remember the pact," and, of course, I said "remember the pact" back. I don't want her to doubt me ever again.

Smellika spent the rest of the day in her PE shorts. She didn't try to make eye contact with any of us during practice, like before. She didn't even bother calling out "Hey, Peyton" this morning like she always does.

The *Beacon* came out today. There's a great photo on my "Last Look" page of me basing with Lexie on my shoulders. Compular took the picture. I've never seen him without his camera. He's always snapping pictures at people when they're not looking.

His tutoring session already paid off. I got a seventy on my trig quiz today! Okay, so I'm not ready to be a mathlete just yet, but it's a huge improvement from a fifty-eight. He can't believe I'm so happy to get a seventy. I hugged him and thanked him in drama. I would never hug him in public, in the halls, but I don't care what the drama people think. Maya was watching us. When she realized I saw her, she looked away. I'm sure she's dying of curiosity to know what I was hugging him about.

Lexie drove me home again today, even though I live right behind campus. Beth Ann's been out with Justin every day after school, so I sat in her usual seat. I saw people noticing us when we drove off. I felt like a star!

In the car, Lexie offered me a cigarette. I tried to say no, but she lit it up anyway, steering the car with her knee. I pretended to puff, but mostly just held it. She didn't come up to the apartment, thank God, but she must know about my money situation now from seeing my building. It's not exactly Trump Tower.

We lost a game again. Hunter kept throwing bad passes. He's the worst player on the team.

Two emails from Sk8man (Von) today! The dance is eight days away!

SATURDAY, SEPTEMBER 18.

Had lunch with Uncle Jeb and Mom at Pizza Hut. When we left, I saw Dorkowitz and Tim Ishikawa walking out of Lee Academy of Martial Arts, which is right next to Pizza Hut. They were wearing those white karate pajamas. They didn't see me. I can't imagine Dorkowitz yelling and kicking, or chopping wood with his bare hands. That makes as much sense as Griffin in wrestling tights.

SUNDAY, SEPTEMBER 19.

Lexie sent the whole squad an email. She signed it "RTP." It took me a while to figure out that "RTP" stands for "Remember the Pact." The email was about Cemetery Night. We're doing it Saturday night, after the dance. We all have an assignment. Lexie's going to get Smellika and bring her to the cemetery at midnight. She has to sleep there in a sleeping bag. I could never do it. I firmly believe in ghosts. I won't even play with a Ouija board.

Some of us have to bring ketchup for Devin and Beth Ann so they can pour it all over themselves. They're going to dress like corpses and jump out from behind gravestones. My job is to stand on the corner with Carmen and

Marisol. We have to make sure no one sets foot on the cemetery grounds once the prank starts. It's really important we're on time.

There's a fist in my stomach every time I think about what they're going to do to Smellika. At least I don't have to be that directly involved. I'm just a guard. The main thing I'm worried about is being late, or messing up my date with Von. He'll have to bring me there after I watch him play with his band. I hope he doesn't get mad.

Lexie already spoke to Mrs. Garret, telling her we're going to have a campout with the whole squad sleeping under the stars at a park. She made it sound like a girl scout retreat type of thing. If she only knew her daughter will be alone all night in a cemetery…

Lexie says that if we check off a few more items on the list this week, Smellika may drop out before Saturday, and if that happens, we may not even have to go through with Cemetery Night at all.

That's what I'm hoping for. The threat of losing my scholarship if I get caught being involved in any of this is hanging over me like a black cloud. The others probably just worry about getting suspended, or being on athletic probation.

I have a lot more to lose.

Monday, September 20.

We had a JV line-up after practice in the locker room. Lexie made all the JV girls stand on a bench in their bras and underwear for a liposuction check. It was their punishment for using the showers before us and leaving us with the cold water. Their hair was still wet and they were all shivering.

Smellika had to get up there with them, too. The JV girls all inched away from her, like they might catch something. It could have been her b.o., which is staggering right after practice. Juretha, Beth Ann, Devin, and Pinky took out lipsticks and circled all the places where they need lipo. Lexie shined a laser flashlight (she had it attached to her key chain) on spots they missed.

"Come on, you too, Peyton," Juretha said, handing her lipstick to me. "Do Smellika." I painted circles around the bluish cellulite on Smellika's thighs. She was shaking like crazy and biting her lip, trying not to cry. Her expression made me want to cry. There she was, trying to stay proud while a bunch of pretty girls underlined her ugliness by marking up her body, demanding that she feel inferior to us. It was so wrong.

And I knew it better than anybody.

I had a flashback of last year in JV, when I was in a line-up. Lexie called it a boob ranking. We had to take off our bras and line up from smallest to largest. I was second in line. Only Pinkie had smaller breasts than me. I still remember how low I felt when Devin said, "I've seen better knobs on doors" after I took off my bra, and then hearing the varsity girls laugh their heads off. Everybody forgot about that line-up after a few days, but not me. For weeks,

I walked around feeling ashamed. And it's probably just a fraction of what Smellika felt.

What we did today was worse than the boob ranking. It was an attack. Beth Ann even drew on her face. I never finished drawing the circles on her legs. I just gave Juretha her lipstick back and went to the bathroom. I needed to get out of there. Carmen and Marisol were mad at themselves because they didn't think to film it with their phones, and wouldn't it have made the best viral video on YouTube?

Smellika was so covered in lipstick she had to shower again afterward instead of just smearing it off like the others. She used the private shower stall (the only one she ever uses—she never uses the open showers like the rest of us) probably thinking she'd finally be left alone. But Devin banged on the door the whole time she was in there and threw toilet paper rolls over the door, yelling, "Bombs away!" and "Don't slip!"

When she ran out of toilet paper, Lexie and a few others threw sweatshirts and socks from the lost and found crate. The only time they stopped was when Coach Wisser came into the locker room to go to her office. Everyone went "sshhh" and got quiet. But the minute Coach Wisser's door was closed, they started throwing stuff again. I sat on the bench and told Lexie I had cramps. It wasn't a lie.

Coach Wisser must have a soundproof office because it got pretty loud. You'd think she'd come out to see what was happening, but she never did. I'm starting to wonder about her. She's always been nice and fun and everything, but doesn't she have any idea? Is she deaf? Pretending? Putting her head in the sand? I don't get it.

TUESDAY, SEPTEMBER 21.

Von gave me a present today! My first present from a guy. He said he forgot to bring it yesterday. It's a shark-tooth necklace. He bought it last weekend in Cocoa Beach, where he was surfing with his friends. He also got the same one for himself. I actually picked up the phone to tell Maya about it, and was even dialing her number, when it hit me that we're not friends anymore. I miss having someone I can tell everything to. I miss having a best friend. I miss Maya's laugh.

I will never take this necklace off. Except at bedtime. Because it might hurt if it pokes me in my sleep.

He was waiting for me at my locker when I got to school and we walked to class holding hands. I can't stop looking at him when I'm with him. It's like I want to memorize every part of his face: his sunburnt nose, his dark green eyes, his full lips, the way his hair falls across his forehead.

Operation Smellika is still moving forward. Shawntay and Kaitlyn have been leaving her phone messages and sending emails every day, telling her she's disgusting and that everybody hates her and we'll rearrange her face if she doesn't drop out of varsity. Juretha got hold of Smellika's cell phone and changed the ring tone to some X-rated rap song, then Juretha called Smellika's phone a million times during the community service assembly. Smellika kept trying to get her phone back to turn it off, but Juretha passed it around from row to row. It blasted every curse word for private parts over and over again. When Dr. Johnson asked who's phone it was and Smellika had to stand up and say it was hers, she got detention.

I wish she would just drop out already and this could all be over. She never tries to make eye contact with any of us anymore, and during practice she stays in the back, quiet, trying to be invisible. Rumor has it her mother hired a private coach, trying to help her with dance moves and jumps.

I wonder how much Mrs. Garret knows. She can't know much, or I'm sure we'd all have been called into Coach Wisser's office by now. I've seen her in the PTO office a lot, and her daughter's always there with her even though students aren't supposed to be allowed in. I almost never see Smellika at our lockers anymore, not since the day I stepped on her glasses.

I had a dream about it the other day. I stepped on her glasses and in my dream the whole school was there, watching and clapping. Dr. Johnson took me away in handcuffs and put me in a squad car. When the car started driving away, the policeman driving turned around and it was Smellika! And she was crying and pointing at me and crying and crying. I woke up in a sweat with my heart pounding on high speed, up in my throat, like when I stuff too many towels into the washing machine and it goes crazy on the spin cycle, banging against the wall like it's about to blast off into space.

WEDNESDAY, SEPTEMBER 22.

I'm so excited! After practice, Lexie drove me to the mall where we met up with Carmen, Marisol, Devin, and Juretha. And guess what? We all got our belly buttons pierced! Lexie totally talked the guy out of the consent forms. We didn't have to show ID or sign anything, probably because she took out her platinum card and told us to pick out whatever. I got a dangling blue stone, just like I wanted! It looks so hot. I have to hide it from Mom, though. She will totally freak.

Pavlich's class isn't that fun anymore. I've even considered doing some actual work in there to tune out what's going on. This whole Smellika thing is making me break out. I have two mammoth zits on my chin. They better disappear by Saturday!

Dr. Giles checked journals today to make sure we're writing in them. She didn't read anything. She just let me flip the pages around to show her I've been keeping up with it, then said, "Excellent. Excellent. You have filled pages with your thoughts. You are a great observer of people. But are you an observer of yourself?"

I'm confused. She's like Buddha. Or is it Confucius? Dr. Giles says she wants to stage an alternate ending to *Julius Caesar*, in which the senators are women who don't resort to violence. Personally, I think audiences would rather see him get stabbed.

Smellika's locker was full of ants today. I don't know who put them there, but I'm just glad Lexie didn't pick me to do it. This prank sucked for me. My locker got infested with ants that traveled over from Smellika's, and so did a few other kids'. We all had to take our stuff out so the maintenance people could spray. Now all my books reek and there are dead ants on everything. Compular's trig notes are ruined.

Smellika's locker got sprayed first. She had some half-eaten granola bars that were covered with hundreds of ants. It was repulsive. A paperback called *How to Talk to People: The Art of Making Friends* was covered too. The thought that she's been reading a self-help book while we've been doing all these horrible things to her is too pitiful for words.

After the maintenance people finished spraying they wiped down the inside of our lockers, but we had to stay and wipe off our books. They gave us paper towels, spray cleaner, and garbage bags. The other kids complained that for what this school costs, the janitors should have been the ones cleaning our stuff, and the school is going to hear from their parents.

Dr. Johnson patrolled the halls just like he did on the jumbo-panties day. Only this time he wasn't with a security guard, he was with Mrs. Garret. She was boiling mad. She said something like, "I want answers. This is an outrage. I didn't invest in this school to put up with vandalism and harassment. I demand that you expel the juvenile delinquent responsible for this."

My blood ran cold when she said that last part. What if they think I did it? My locker is right next to Smellika's. Plus, it had to be someone in on the pact, and I'm part of it.

Every time Dr. Johnson tried to answer her, she cut him off and yelled some more. I've never seen anyone treat our principal like a little boy who just wet his pants. He kept gesturing toward the main office, trying to steer her out of the hallway. But she wouldn't budge.

Smellika was standing there, too, and this time she didn't care who saw her crying. Probably because there weren't that many people around to notice her. Lexie and all the Alphas had gone to class. I was focused on wiping off my books and throwing away ruined papers, and the other kids were busy too, cleaning, grumbling quietly to each other, and trying to eavesdrop on Mrs. Garret ripping Dr. Johnson a new one. No one was paying any attention to Smellika.

But when I glanced up for a second and saw her, something came over me. It was the way she was standing all slumped over next to her mother, almost like she was trying to be a shadow. It was the way the tears slid down her face, and the way her pathetic *How to Talk to People* book was all ruined and spotted with dead ants. I wanted to do something for her, for once. Something nice.

So I wiped down some of her stuff. I only wiped the stuff that didn't have too many ants, like her book and a few folders. I know she saw me doing it, but she wouldn't look directly at me. I wanted to tell her I didn't do this, that I was sorry. But maybe by helping her clean up a little, she knows that.

Lexie told me to move my stuff into her locker because she has an extra shelf. So my new locker is right near Sloane, Juretha, Devin, and Beth Ann, in the senior section! Now I'll get to hang out with them in between classes like a true, official Alpha.

Dr. Johnson called an assembly for eighth period. I sat next to Von, A.J. and Mike. Dr. Johnson started off by saying, "I am fed up with the latest shenanigans here, and I am determined to find and punish those responsible." He was wearing his navy and white checkered sport coat. His voice was a little more animated than usual, like he might actually have a pulse. "Beachwood is committed to upholding the highest standards of behavior and respect, and any student found to be in violation of those standards will face dire consequences."

Everyone was buzzing about the ant invasion, trying to figure out who did it. They were all blaming Griffin. He's an obvious choice. But he's not in on the pact. Von and Mike kept looking at each other, mumbling. Did Von have something to do with it?

Then I remembered. At the bonfire on the beach, Mike said his sister had an ant colony. *She won't miss it ...* And Von had jumped at the chance to lend a hand. *Dude, I'll do it with you.* I watched them during the assembly. They were snickering and laughing quietly whenever anybody made a comment about the ants. It bothered me that Von was laughing. I thought about it all day. I've done mean things to Smellika, too, but I never laughed about it later.

FRIDAY, SEPTEMBER 24.

We finally won a game tonight! Our new cheer went great, too: *Touchdown, touchdown, score, score, score, Beachwood sharks, score some more, kill, kill, kill, Beachwood sharks, S-H-A-R-K-S! KILL, KILL, KILL!!!* Even Smellika did okay with it. I think she's been practicing a lot. The only time she made us look stupid was when we all rippled down into splits. She couldn't do it, so she just sank down and put one leg forward. It ruined the ripple.

But I give her credit for showing up at all. She never made it to yesterday's practice after the ant incident. And she must know we're the ones who did it. It takes guts for her to face us every day, knowing we're out to get her. I don't know how she does it.

Her mom was there tonight, and so was her father, Lord Garret himself. Why doesn't she say anything to her parents? She could turn us all in if she wanted to. It boggles the mind.

Von didn't come. He emailed me a picture of himself doing a skate trick called a melon.

18

Tonight's the night. Lexie and I are riding back to her house, top down, Lil' Kim blasting, cigarettes dangling from our fingers. Lexie showed up at my building this morning. I was in the back lot practicing my tumbling, which is pretty weak compared to the rest of the squad. I was so caught off guard to see her, I fell in the middle of my handspring and whacked my head.

"Your mom told me you were out here," she laughed, all bronzed and beautiful. She was wearing a halter top and cut-offs.

"You saw my apartment?" I was planning on hiding it from her forever.

"Yeah, your crib is cute," she said. Then she told me we were getting manicures. When I told her I do my own, she just said, "not today," and the next thing I knew we were at her nail salon, where I learned that the latest take on

French manicures is the trendy new black tip. Which Lexie and I both got (courtesy of Lexie's platinum credit card).

Now she's taking me to her house for lunch. Her cook made sushi. Everyone on the squad keeps calling her cell phone. They're all worked up about the dance and Cemetery Night.

"Right after lunch, I'll take you home," Lexie says, screeching to stop for a red light. I'm getting used to her driving. "We both need time to nap. It's going to be a late night, you know."

I smile and pretend to inhale my cigarette. "And tomorrow..."

We both say it at the same time. "No more Smellika!" The light turns green. Lexie hits the gas and the car speeds toward her house. I throw my hands up, Superman style, as if I could fly.

~ ~ ~

Her kitchen takes up three rooms, if you count the pantry. Everything is chrome and black granite. There's a tray of sushi and two plates laid out for us on a counter. I've never eaten sushi and it looks icky, but I act like I'm really happy to eat it because Lexie keeps saying, "I love sushi. This sushi is the best," etc. I pull out a stool from under the counter and sit. Lexie fills her plate, but she eats standing up, leaning against the wall.

I'm putting these weird rice rolls on my plate when the swinging door blows open and Lexie's mother storms in. She's wearing the same shoes as last time, the ones with the crystals.

And nothing else.

I look down at my plate, thinking she'll run out to put some clothes on. But she doesn't leave, and she's definitely not embarrassed. "I thought I heard noises in here," she says like she's discovered rodents raiding her garbage. Lexie doesn't move or speak. My eyes stay glued to my plate. But I can still see Mrs. Court put her hand on her hip and walk over to me and Lexie. "Well, well, well. Look who's here." I smell alcohol.

I have to look. She's standing right in front of me, completely naked. I can't help myself. I look. Her flesh is as white and smooth as an egg. Her breasts are small and hard. Lexie sees me looking and I quickly glance away. I stay very still, perched on my stool, trying to fade into the background like a chameleon.

Lexie's not moving, either. I can hear her breathing through her nose. "Why are you here? You're supposed to be in South Beach this weekend," she says with quiet pain in her voice. It strikes me that if her mother wasn't naked, Lexie wouldn't be so timid. She'd probably be all angry like the last time.

"So happy to see you too, dearest," her mother sneers, opening a cabinet. She takes out a bottle of something clear. I think it's vodka. Her Manolo Blahniks are giving her some trouble with balance. An invisible wind is making her sway back and forth. "I know how you just *love* for me to meet your friends." I guess she doesn't remember she's met me before. Her eyes are glassy and half-closed. I'm afraid she's going to drop the vodka. The bottle is pretty loose in her hand. She weaves her way over to the fridge and takes out a container of orange juice, then shuts the door with her elbow.

The swinging doors open again. It's Mrs. Court's friend, the one with the Cleopatra hair, wearing panties and a tank top. She nods at us and says, "Good morning," even though it's one in the afternoon.

"Here, Lorna, take these back to the bedroom," Mrs. Court says in the same commanding voice Lexie uses when she's ordering us to do something. Lorna takes the o.j. and vodka and leaves.

Suddenly, Lexie springs into action. "Let's go," she says to me, reaching for her keys on the counter.

But quick as a cat, her mother snatches the keys away and throws them across the huge kitchen. "No. Stay." She chuckles, which makes her pale belly quiver. A few fast steps, and now she's pressed herself against Lexie, pinning her daughter's back to the wall. They're nose to nose. With her hands high above Lexie's head, palms pressed flat on the wall, she uses her body as a trap. Lexie is boxed in.

"Mother, please," Lexie begs, turning her head to the side, probably to escape her mother's alcohol breath. "Stop this. Go get dressed." Her face has an expression I've never seen before. She looks scared. That makes me scared, too.

Mrs. Court speaks directly into Lexie's ear. "You really

think you're something, don't you?" Lexie winces. "Don't you?" Lexie squeezes her eyes shut. "Well. You. Are. Nothing." A few seconds pass. Neither one moves a muscle. "Do you hear me?" She backs away a little. "You're nothing." She pokes Lexie in the chest with each word. "And you always will be."

The swinging door is still flapping back and forth after she leaves. Not once did that woman look at me or acknowledge my presence. Lexie is still sucked to the wall in the same position, her eyes tightly shut. I want to hug her or touch her arm, comfort her in some way, but I can't. Lexie is untouchable.

I want to tell her to forget everything her mother said, that she's a drunk, that she's the one who's nothing. I want to tell her that her mother needs serious help. Mostly, I want to escape this place. I'm sure Lexie does too. I go and get her keys off the floor. She opens her eyes.

I hold out the keys. She stares at them for a minute, then scoops them out of my hand and runs out the side door, down to the beach. I follow her.

~ ~ ~

We're sitting on the sand hugging our knees. She won't look at me. She hasn't said a word. Neither have I. Neither of us knows what to say. She's pouring sand into piles with her hand, over and over. She doesn't even care about ruining her manicure. Words don't seem appropriate right now. We just listen to the whoosh of the waves and watch the sea.

After a long time, she says, "You didn't see any of that,

okay? She's in South Beach this weekend. She's staying at the Delano Hotel. None of this happened."

"Okay."

"You won't tell?"

"Tell what? Nothing happened."

Lexie looks so relieved, she almost smiles. Sand slips through her fingers, making wavy designs. "She's been surprising me like that lately. Being here when she's not supposed to be." She gazes up at the sky, watching some seagulls. "Not even Beth Ann or Hunter know everything about…about…" She stops, searching for words. "I'm a very private person, you know?"

"I know." She nods and meets my eyes. They're full of words she's not saying. She's trusting me with a huge secret that no one else knows. And it's not about her mother's drinking or her mother's love life.

It's about the fact that her own mother hates her. She's worried I'll let the ugly truth slip out. Then Lexie Court won't be perfect anymore. Because how can the whole school love a girl her own mother despises?

"Don't worry," I tell her. It's all I can say. It sounds crazy, but I feel privileged to be the only one who knows, to be the keeper of Lexie Court's deepest, darkest secret. We'll always have that bond between us now.

She looks out to sea. Her dark brown eyes are soft. Now's the time to ask the question everybody's whispered since fourth grade. "Where's your father?"

She makes a new design in the sand before answering.

"I'm not sure. Martinique, I think. Or St. Barths. I'll find out at Christmas when he sends my check." Then, "I wonder if he'll send a picture of the baby."

"Baby?"

The sand is very important now. She's drawing lines in it. "Yup. His girlfriend was pregnant last Christmas, so she must have had the baby by now." She concentrates on her designs, making swirls and circles. I have a million questions, like, are your parents divorced, is the baby a boy or a girl? But this is Lexie. I keep quiet and wait to see if she still feels like letting her walls come down.

She doesn't. She rubs her hands together briskly, getting the sand off of them. The spell is broken. "Listen, forget we ever had this little chat, okay? Like I said, my mother is in South Beach, and my father is, uh, let's see—"

"Away on business?"

"Right. Away on business." She tosses her keys in the air, catches them with one hand, gets up, brushes the sand off her knees. "Time to go home and get some rest, Prairie Girl. Between the dance and Cemetery Night, we have a lot to do."

19

I can't rest, not after what I've witnessed at Lexie's. I just get ready, choosing earrings and laying out my new jeans, chiffon top, favorite flip-flops, and purse with a bottle of ketchup in it. Mom blends concealer over my two zits, because they've morphed into another chin. Before this afternoon, I probably would have been annoyed with her help, but right now I'm feeling like I won the mom lottery. I hug her when she's done. It confuses her. "You okay, Junebug?"

"Yeah. I'm good."

We wait out front because I don't want Von to see our apartment. He's so polite to Mom and Uncle Jeb (who just happened to drop by) that I can't get over it. I was worried he'd greet them in his native surfer/skater tongue, but he's using phrases like "pleased to meet you" and "ma'am" and "sir," giving strong handshakes. He could pass for a prep if it wasn't for his earring and the newly sprouted soul patch under his lip.

The ride to the dance is so uncomfortable, it's like body snatchers have taken away our ability to flirt. If our conversation was a script in Dr. Giles' class, it would look like this:

VON: Your mom looks like that chick from all those old movies, whatshername?
PEYTON: Molly Ringwald?
VON: Yeah, that one.

Extremely awkward silence. Peyton takes off the sweater that hides her belly ring. She waits for a compliment from Von. He says nothing. He doesn't even tell her she looks pretty.

PEYTON: So the dance should be really good tonight.
VON: Uh-huh. Should be.

Another extremely awkward silence. The car stops for a red light. Von leans over and explores Peyton's mouth with his long tongue. He's stretching her jaw so much, Peyton is sure it will separate, the way a snake's jaw does before swallowing a rat. His lips slide all over the bottom half of her face. The light turns green. Peyton daintily wipes the saliva from around her lips with her discarded sweater. She's gotten lipstick all over it. More silence.

Good thing I live around the corner from school, so this wordless abyss only lasts about two minutes. It hasn't occurred to me before, but Von and I have never had a real conversation. The most we've said to each other is through emails.

The cafetorium is decorated with barrels and hay-stacks. Strobe lights flash over the packed dance floor. Von and I watch as a teacher interrupts a couple that's grinding, and makes them stop.

It's fun to see everyone out of uniform, in jeans and overalls. Some of the sluttier girls are wearing tiny cut-offs, à la Daisy Duke. My outfit is perfect, I think, judging from the looks I'm getting from Von. He's got his arm around me.

A.J. struts up to us. Mike is behind him. I don't think they have dates. "Dawg, you made it," A.J. says to Von. They barely nod at me. Mike says he has to show Von something outside.

"Be right back," Von says. "Two secs. That's all." Then he's gone. I try to ignore this heavy feeling coming over me. We just got here and already he's out the door?

Lexie and Beth Ann are dancing with Hunter and Justin. Shawntay and Raquel are dancing with guys I've never seen. They must be from another school. Von better get back soon. We should be on the dance floor too.

Lexie looks fantastic in a denim mini and snakeskin cowboy boots. So much for the jeans she told us she was going to wear. Her smiling face doesn't reveal any of the horrific events from today. Anybody watching her just sees a happy, glamorous diva. If only people knew what I know.

I feel stupid standing here. This isn't the way I pictured

my date. He was supposed to ask me if I want to dance or if I want a drink, not run off with his buddies the first chance he gets. I go to a dark corner, far from the dance floor. Let Von find me.

"Hey, where's your drink?" It's Compular. He's got two cups of punch, one in each hand.

"Don't have one yet. Where's your camera? You here for the *Beacon?*"

"No. I was invited, thank you very much. And don't look so surprised."

"Sorry. By who?"

"Kim Wu."

"She's nice. Where is she?"

"In the bathroom. What's with girls and the bathroom? You go in groups and stay there forever. What do you girls do in there?"

"I could tell you, but then I'd have to kill you. It's a global conspiracy."

"That important, huh? I was hoping it was just sexual."

"No such luck."

"So what about you? Who's the lucky guy?"

"Von Cohen." My eyes scan around, searching for him. "He, uh, had to step out for a sec," I explain.

"Hey, can I ask you a question?"

"Sure."

"What's your middle name?"

My eyes narrow. "Why?"

"For the *Beacon*. I've been putting people's full names for photo credit lately. Makes the picture more interesting."

"I don't have a middle name."

"Liar." He looks up at me, smiling his dopey smile with his big dimples popping out. "Maya told me you wouldn't tell." So Maya didn't give it away. She's still loyal. It's nice to know. "She said it's top secret."

I need to change the subject. I point to one of his cups. "Can I have a punch?"

"Sure." He puts the cups on the floor and punches me lightly in the arm. I stare at him. He punches me again. "You asked for it," he says. Giggles escape me, beyond my control. It is such a typical, stupid Compular joke. I don't know why I'm laughing. We both are. "Want another one?" He punches me again.

I punch him back. "Here's one for you, because your jokes are so lame."

Someone taps my shoulder. It's Von. "You guys are always, like, Comedy Central," he says, sounding far away. Mike and A.J. are behind him.

Compular's suddenly in a hurry. "Better go find Kim." He picks the cups up. "See ya later."

"Say hi for me," I call after him, even though I don't know Kim very well.

"Who's Kim?" asks Von, gazing upward with red, glassy eyes. He's mesmerized by the flashing lights above us.

Great. He's stoned.

~ ~ ~

"We need to discuss her outfit," Lexie says, perched above us all on the window ledge. Beth Ann and Devin are leaning against the sinks, smoking. Sloane and Pinkie are putting on lipstick. Lexie's email said to meet in the bathroom by the theater because it's always empty. We're supposed to hand over our ketchup and go over our jobs for tonight.

I keep waiting for Lexie to give me a secret signal, some kind of look or gesture to show we're a little closer after today, that I'm in on something the others aren't. But it's not happening. She's still calling me "Prairie Girl" and giving me cigarettes, but there's no sign of friendship, no sign of what happened with her mother or the talk we had. She's buried it.

She doesn't feel any closer to me. I was so sure we'd have a stronger bond after her confessions to me this afternoon, but she's back to keeping me at a safe distance, pretending I never caught a glimpse of the underside of her sparkling life.

I miss the comfort of Maya. Sometimes I don't feel like I have a true friend in the squad. We're together a lot, but we're not in on each other's feelings and thoughts that much. I always thought everybody had a tight connection with their best friend, but Beth Ann and Lexie don't. They don't act like best friends, the way they treat each other. They're more like best frenemies.

The rest of the squad already came and left. They didn't want to keep their dates waiting. I wish my date felt that way. Von's been disappearing on and off all night. I don't even know where he is right now. I'm feeling so low, and there's no one I can talk about it with, even though I'm surrounded by my so-called friends.

Sloane is telling us about the restaurant she went to for dinner, some fancy steak house Diego drove all the way from Miami to take her to. Von didn't even buy me a coke, let alone dinner. My hopes and dreams for this night are crushed.

I don't even want to see him in his stupid band. Except that at the club, he might be different and pay more attention to me. For all I know, I'm expecting too much. It could be that he's too stoned to realize how crappy he's treating me, or he hates dances. I had imagined us slow dancing, talking, laughing together. I wanted everyone to see Von Cohen by my side all night, with eyes only for me. Instead, his eyes aren't for anybody because they're barely open from all the weed he's been smoking in the parking lot with his sidekicks.

I'm miserable. At times like these, I ache to talk to Maya. She'd see things clearly. She'd know how I should handle it.

"Comments about her *très chic ensemble?*" asks Lexie, crossing her legs. She's referring to Smellika's brown overalls. Smellika is here, at the dance, behind the popcorn table with her mother and the other parent volunteers.

"Yeah, what is she supposed to be, the brown M&M?" asks Beth Ann.

"No," I say, "more like a brown ..." I blow out smoke, buying time, trying to think of something funny that's brown. "A brown ..."

Devin finishes my sentence: "Doody." Peals of laughter bounce off the tile floors.

"I spoke to her an hour ago, reminding her to be ready to go at midnight," Lexie says when the noise dies down.

"What exactly did you tell her about tonight's little activity?" Sloane asks.

"That it's a sleepover with the whole JV squad, and that she has to go through the same mandatory initiation rituals as they do, since she's a newbie. I told her she'll be picked up out front at ten of twelve and taken to a private location."

Sloane doesn't seem satisfied. "What are you going to tell her when she doesn't see any JV girls there?"

"That they're on their way."

"I don't think she'll believe it," says Beth Ann.

"Do me a favor, B.A. Try not to think." Lexie fluffs out her hair. "You'll only hurt yourself." Beth Ann shoots Lexie a *screw you* look, but doesn't dare say it.

"Does she seem scared?" Pinkie wants to know, looking pretty scared herself.

Lexie blows smoke rings. "Hard to tell. I played up the whole trust exercise, bonding angle, like the guys did. She thinks that after tonight, she'll be one of us."

"When monkeys fly out of my ass," Devin says.

Sloane touches one of the appliqués on my pocket. "I am loving your Chip and Pepper jeans, Peyton."

"Thanks." I knew they were hot. Lexie and Beth Ann have been eyeballing them all night. I'll bet one of them will ask me where I got them. I'll say Bloomingdale's.

Sure enough, Lexie asks me. "Where'd you get them?"

"Bloomie's."

"I didn't see those at Bloomie's," she says.

"Me neither," says Beth Ann. She and Lexie trade funny smiles.

I can handle this. "Oh, wait. These? That's right. I didn't get these at Bloomie's. I was thinking of another pair. These I got at a boutique in Palm Beach." It's not so far from the truth. I think they believe me.

"What's the boutique called?" Lexie must really want these jeans.

I throw up my hands and knock on my head. "I wish I could remember. It was such a long time ago."

"If you remember the name, let me know." Lexie locks eyes with Beth Ann, who says, "Yeah, let us know." Maybe they're competing to see who gets them first. Frenemies.

"I will."

Lexie drops her cigarette, jumps down from the ledge and crushes it out with her foot. "We better get back to the *soirée*. Without us, it's not a party." Everyone files out after her. "Remember to be on time tonight."

I stay behind to pee, and also because I know they're all going to their devoted dates. I don't want to be embarrassed if they realize Von has better things to do than hang out with me.

I'm alone in the stall. Someone comes in. I flush and come out.

It's Smellika.

20

I walk past her as if she's not there, turn on the tap, squirt out some soap. "Hey, Peyton," she says.

"Hey."

"I wanted to thank you."

I wash my hands as if preparing for surgery. I'm too nervous to talk to her. Lexie may have left, but her presence is still in this bathroom, watching me.

"For wiping off my stuff. I saw you, you know, the day with the ants."

"You're welcome." She sneezes a few times. I don't say bless you. There are no paper towels and I don't have time for the hand dryer. I wipe my hands on my jeans and head for the exit. I need to get out of here fast, before someone walks in and sees me talking to her.

"Peyton." I'm at the door. *Keep walking, Peyton, go, go, go.*

Something in her voice makes me stop. "I've got to know something," she says to my back. "It's about tonight."

"I can't tell you anything. You know that."

"Just tell me if there's really going to be a sleepover. Please. If it's another trick, I need to know." Long seconds pass. The faucet is dripping. The fluorescent lights hum. "Are you guys going to hurt me? I just want to be prepared."

Are we going to hurt her? *Are we going to hurt her?* I turn around to see if she's kidding. Doesn't she get it by now? Of course we're going to hurt her. We hurt her until she drops out. It's simple. We've spelled it out, day after day.

She's not kidding. She's so clueless, I don't know whether to hug or slap her. How can she not comprehend where this is all going?

I throw my words like darts. "You have to quit the squad." She falls back against the sinks, as if I've pushed her. "Drop out. Go tell Lexie you're quitting. Now."

"I c-can't."

"Why? Why the hell not?" I can't keep the anger out of my voice.

"Because this was all my idea."

"What was?"

"Everything. My parents investing in this school, me being a cheerleader. I put them up to it. No more ellie-phant jokes."

"Ellie-phant?"

"Here, I'm Smellika. At Palm Glades Prep, I was Ellie-phant." God, that's horrible. For all her millions, no one would ever want to trade places with her. "I told my parents everybody likes cheerleaders," she says quickly, probably afraid I'll run out any second. "They thought it was a great idea. I can't tell them now, after everything they've done, all the money—" Her voice cracks. She stops, controls it. "I can't tell them it's worse here than at my other school. How could I do that?"

Her nose is turning red. "I think my mom knows. I've been trying to hide it, but she's starting to see. I know she sees now." She stomps her foot and talks to the ceiling. "Just once, I want to make them proud, finish something I've started, you know?"

So Smellika has a plan, too. Who knew? But it doesn't matter. She'll have to drop out eventually, no matter how much it will disappoint her parents. Can't she see that, after everything she's been through, how the hazing just gets worse and worse?

A tear trickles down from under her glasses. She pulls a tissue out of her pocket and wipes it away. "I can't quit. Never, ever. No matter what you all do to me." This girl is in denial. Newsflash for Ellika Garret: you're up against Lexie Court. You won't win. You'll quit whether you want to or not.

She blows her nose, a real honker, loud and gross. "Besides, some day you guys will get tired of picking on me." There's hope in her sad voice.

No, Smellika. Someday you'll get tired of being picked on, that's how this thing works.

It all makes sense to me now, why she puts up with all of it, from the ants to the website pictures to Pavlich's class. And why she'll keep putting up with hazing abuse for another semester: to star in another episode of *The Popular Cheerleading Daughter Show* for her parents. And because, somehow, she actually believes we'll stop hounding her some day.

Guilt stabs me everywhere. "How do you take it?"

She waits a while before answering. "Some days, I don't know."

"I stepped on your glasses. I stole your uniform. Why are you talking to me?"

She shrugs. "You look me in the eye. Not always, but sometimes. The others never do." I try to remember if I've ever seen anyone make eye contact with her. "It's true. They look me up and down, make fun of me as if I were a picture of a person instead of a real, live person. They never really look at me the way you do."

I look in her eyes now, magnified under her glasses. They're full of anxiety, searching my face, reaching out. "Is it really just a JV sleepover, an initiation thing, like Lexie said?" Our reflections are multiplied in the mirrors over the sinks. Me, with my hands in my pockets, Smellika with her pudgy palms pressed together in a praying position, the used tissue smushed between them. "Please tell me if anything bad's going to happen, Peyton. Please."

A beehive is swarming in my brain. Thoughts sting me so fast I can't keep up. I want to tell her the truth. It's on the tip of my tongue. *They're going to take you to Mullins Cemetery and scare the bejesus out of you until you cry like a baby and wet your pants. And yes, they'll hurt you. Save yourself! Drop out now!*

But it wouldn't be worth it. She won't listen. She said she'd never quit.

If I tell her about tonight, she might just decide to ditch Lexie and go home with her mother. That's bad enough, but the worst she could do is rat me out. Then the whole squad will know I told her and ruined Cemetery Night. Lexie and the others would never forgive me.

I'd be digging my own grave if I even give her so much as a hint, screwing myself. I can't do it. "Of course it's just a sleepover," I say. "Nothing bad's going to happen."

Her face relaxes. She's relieved. *Stop feeling sorry for her. Remember the pact. Sometimes you have to be a bitch to get what you want.* I can't help her. Operation Smellika is in progress. The wheels are in motion.

And I'm a cog in those wheels, just like the rest of the squad. "No, nothing bad's going to happen." I reach for the door. "And we never had this conversation. Don't talk to me again."

I need to finish what I've started, too, Ellika.

~ ~ ~

Von is watching me dance with Carmen and Marisol. It turns out they came together, no dates. That's what Von should have done with his friends. He sure as hell didn't need me around. Mike and A.J. left for Club Hole. Earlier, I found Von outside with them, skateboarding off the wheelchair ramp. This isn't even a disaster date. It's a non-date.

But what if I've been playing it all wrong tonight? What if he wanted me to follow him around and sit on the steps watching him skate, even if he didn't say so? Guys are hard to read; all the magazines say so.

A slow song comes on. He doesn't make any move to come over. I dance over to him. "You want to dance?"

"Nah, let's go somewhere. Get to know each other better." His lips slide into a half-smile, sleepy eyes looking right into mine. Flutter, tingle, shivers everywhere. He's ready to be with me now. Maybe we can start over.

Maybe there's hope for this night after all.

~ ~ ~

The back of his SUV is roomier than it looks. I have plenty of leg room, as long as I bend my legs around the case of beer. We're lying on our sides, knees touching, each propped up on an elbow. He takes two cans from the case and hands one to me without asking if I want it. It's warm. I can't drink it. "Isn't your band waiting for you?"

"Mike called. Our set's been pushed back. We've got time."

"Don't forget I have to be at the cemetery at twelve."

"Chill. You'll get there." He gulps his beer with loud swallows. I check out my surroundings while he drinks: dream catcher hanging from the rearview mirror with Mardi

Gras beads, two skateboards in the back, a crumpled Tony Hawk T-shirt.

"Why so sub-level, Peyton Cheerleader? You're not drinking your brew." He puts his hand above my knee, rubbing it in circular motions.

I want to ask him why he's been ignoring me, if I did something wrong. But he's paying attention to me now. I'm not going to blow it. I snap open the flip-top and sip some, trying not to gag. "So, what's the name of your band?"

"Fractured Neck."

"How'd you come up with that?"

"I fractured my neck."

"You mean you broke it?"

"Uh-huh. Me and my crew were hanging out boarding one day and I fell off my deck. I was doing a one-eighty and went flying, landed on a step. Then there was this loud crack, scared the piss out of me, totally blacked out." He lets out a guffaw—a Neanderthal, macho laugh—like breaking his neck is the funniest thing ever. Boy humor, I guess.

"Oh my God."

"So I asked the ER doc what was wrong with me, and he goes, 'fractured neck.' My core was really damaged for a sec, but then I went, whoa, fractured neck, sweet name for the band, hyah."

"Did you have to stay in the hospital a long time?"

"Two weeks. And I had to wear this crazy-looking steel trap on my neck and back for six months. Missed a semester. Had to go to summer school twice."

"That must have sucked."

"It did." He covers his mouth with his fist and muffles a burp. A poof of beer vapor floats past me.

Huge, yawning silence. It's like this burst of information filled our conversation quota, and no more words are available at this time. I try to get a little more beer down, then give up and put the can back in the case. He does the same with his.

More quiet nothingness. The air is thick with it. *What to say, what to say...* His hand travels higher. I know he wants to get busy, but I have no idea how to make the move. "My parents met in a band," I suddenly remember. He doesn't need to know it was an ABBA cover band called Abba Nice Day. Mom still has the silver boots.

"For real?"

"Yeah."

He puts his beer back in the case. "Maybe you could do a set with us. You could just go on stage and dance."

"I like that idea."

The hand squeezes my leg. "I like you." He leans forward for a kiss, like an open-mouth bass coming at me. I try to keep up with him, matching his moves, tongue for tongue. His new soul patch is burning the zits on my chin.

Without taking his lips off mine, he rolls on top of me. I wrap my arms around his neck and shoulders. It seems like that's where they should go. His shark tooth necklace, or it might be mine, is puncturing my throat. I don't know about his jaw, but mine is about to dislocate. I want to come up for air, but how?

Hello. His driftwood is awake. He's pumping it against me, back and forth, back and forth. Maya's Bijan Frise humped my leg like this once. I should have made myself drink more beer. He's nibbling my neck. I can breathe now. If only I was enjoying this. My insides might as well be a wad of gum in cold water. There's no flush, no quivers, nothing.

I can't take much more of his mouth gymnastics. My face is exhausted. My chin is killing me. He smells like beer and smoke and sweat. And not in a good way, like the night at the beach. I'm not feeling so in love right now. I briefly wonder if Smellika has ever been kissed, then banish the mental image. Why am I thinking of her now? She always pops up to interrupt me and Von, even in my thoughts.

The hand is back. It's way up my thigh, squeezing, circling, getting closer and closer. Is he going to go *there?*

He does, cupping his hand between my legs and squeezing. Hard. It hurts. I push him off of me, gasping. "Stop." He answers with a groan into my neck and clamps me harder. He thinks I like it. It hurts like hell. "Stop." I don't know much, but I know this is supposed to feel good, not painful. "Stop. Stop."

He stops. "What's wrong?" His breath is terrible.

"It hurts."

"Hurts? What are you, gay?"

"No." *Maybe. Oh no. Am I?*

"Good." He checks his watch. "Cause we've still got time." He flicks up my belly shirt with his index finger. "Let's take a look under the hood." I yank it back down. This is nothing like the romance books I've read. I'm not feeling seduced. I'm feeling groped and grabbed and pushed around. And I'm getting angry. I glare at him. "Okay, okay, relax," he says, hands up in surrender. "We don't have to go there."

He stretches out on his back, puts his hands behind his head, and closes his eyes. Hallelujah. Maybe we're done. He opens one eye at me. What is he doing? The eye closes.

That's when he reaches down and unzips his pants. Real slow, like he's unveiling a great work of art. I sit up, hunched over so I don't bang my head on the roof. "What are you doing?"

"Waiting for you." He pulls his pants down a little, showing me his black boxer shorts. His driftwood is sticking straight up. There's a tattoo on his belly, just above his underwear, a naked lady with football-sized breasts. She's holding a Chinese yin-yang symbol over her head. His belly button is the yang. Or maybe the yin. I'm not sure which.

"To do what?"

He sits up, reaches over, and smooths back my hair. "Come on, Peyton. You know I really like you." His hand slides to the back of my neck, pushing my head down toward his statue of puberty, the way a dog owner forces a puppy's nose into its own shit after it's made on the carpet.

I pull back, smack his hand away. "Cut it out, Von." My teeth are clenched. He's treating me worse than a dog.

Come to think of it, he's treated me lousy for a while. He's never called me once, and his emails are mostly about himself. He's never asked me out. He hasn't even offered me a ride home. And whenever he sees me, all he ever wants to do is turn my mouth into a cave for his fat, slimy tongue.

The only nice thing he's ever done for me is give me the shark tooth necklace, and he bought one for himself, too. He probably got a two-for-one deal. And now, after saying two words to me all night, he automatically expects me to get in his pants?

I grab my purse. All this time, I've been feeling so lucky. I've been such an idiot, the poster child for stupidity.

"Where you going? You said you weren't gay. Prove it." He grins, shooting a gust of air through his nose. Why didn't I ever notice his teeth are the color of cheese? And his nails have dirt under them. I've been blinder than Smellika.

"Why should I? You've been ignoring me since we got here."

"Because I left to smoke a blunt for two minutes?"

"Two minutes? Try all night."

"I wouldn't have had to if you weren't so boring."

"Like riding skateboards with your skeezy friends is so much fun?" His lower lip is hanging open. If he were a cartoon sketch I'd draw a balloon above his head that read, *duh.* "Get a life, you asshole." I open the back hatch and climb out. "You've been treating me like dirt from day one. I'm through with you."

"Through with me? Wait, you're leaving me with a stiffie?"

"Yup."

He's so mad he's speechless. He starts struggling with his zipper, cursing. His pants won't close, and his driftwood is getting smaller. I'm fascinated. Now he's getting even more furious with me for watching him shrink. "Fine. Go." He gives up on the zipper. "And why don't you grow some tits while you're at it, you little tease."

Ouch. Harsh. But I'm not going to let him get away with it. "By the way, just so you know? Your kissing sucks. Royally. Your tongue feels like a slug. You're so bad, it's a joke."

"Like you would know. You've probably never even seen a dick before."

"I've seen you, haven't I?" Funny how we're not at a loss for words anymore. I unclasp the shark-tooth necklace and chuck it clear across the empty parking lot. "You're nothing like I thought you were," I say, almost to myself. He reaches forward and slams the door in my face.

I won't even miss looking at him.

21

I'm late, I'm late, I'm late. That's what my flip-flops are saying with each slap on the sidewalk. I'm late. And in big-time trouble. It's after midnight. A quarter after, to be exact. Von lied to me. I don't know what time I got into his car, but it wasn't early. Bastard. Why did I ever think he was such a great guy? Were aliens controlling my mind?

I haven't looked at a clock all night. Damn, damn, damn. Lexie will rip me to shreds. She told us over and over not to be late. From now on, I'll wear a watch.

Mullins Cemetery is only eight blocks from school. I kick my shoes off, scoop them up, and run. What have I missed, what have they done to Smellika? Her open, trusting face, the way it looked in the bathroom, keeps digging at me.

She thought I was telling the truth. I should have told her. I should have at least given her a hint. By now she knows I lied. Beth Ann and Devin are probably terrorizing her. I run faster.

Thunder roars somewhere above me. Clouds keep passing in front of the moon, causing mini-blackouts. Only weak streetlamps and a few small houses give off any light. I shudder. How anyone could live near a cemetery is beyond me. Just being on this side street makes my skin crawl. It's the trees.

Horror movies always have these kind of trees, tall with twisted trunks. Their branches hang over me now, long, bony arms blowing around, making shadows that jump. The cemetery is full of them. It's on the next block, just ahead.

Carmen, Marisol, Pinky, and Sloane are running toward me. They take turns giving me a play-by-play of what I missed. "Omigod, Peyton, you should see Devin and Beth Ann."

"They're heart-attack scary, I swear. When they came out from behind the trees swinging axes, Smellika went ballistic." A sickening sensation creeps into my gut.

"She screamed at the top of her lungs, took off running. They followed her."

"She didn't even pull her sleeping bag off all the way. One leg was still stuck in it, and it kept dragging behind her. She kept tripping over it."

"Yeah, she couldn't shake it off her leg." The sensation is getting worse.

"We couldn't see where they went. But then we heard

a lot of screams, so we ran in to see what was up, but Devin goes, 'Back to your posts!' And then Lexie yelled at us to forget our posts and just go home."

I hear shouts. They're faint, but I hear them. Pinky hugs herself. "I think they did something in there," she says in her eensie-weensie voice. "They don't want us to see what it is."

What have they done to her?

A loud crack of thunder gives us all a jolt. Sloane jiggles her keys. "Yeah, well, we'll find out later," she says. "This place gives me the creeps." She pushes a button on her key fob. A car parked at the curb chirps. "Let's go."

It's drizzling. The four of them scatter to Sloane's car. Carmen holds the back door open for me. "*Vamos*, Peyton. Hurry, you're getting wet."

I don't care that I'm getting wet. I could have warned Smellika about tonight and I didn't. I sent her here, like a lamb to the slaughter. Now I have to see what the damage is. "There's room for you," Carmen says, pulling the neck of her sweatshirt over her head. It's really starting to come down now. "Come on!"

I shake my head no, and run. There's a sign at the iron gate: *Mullins Cemetery, Est. 1890.* The gate's locked. Easy to climb over. I rip my new chiffon top on the jump down. The screaming and shouting is louder now, but the wind and rain drown out any words.

It's a small cemetery. Streaks of lightning light up row after row of graves. A clap of thunder startles me and I trip over one of the flat gravestones. It's hard to see the foot-path. My feet are sinking into the mud.

Carson, Macallister, Ingalls. The names of the dead follow me. Are they watching me? It's pouring, my wet hair is plastered to my face, and I'm cold and shivering. My top, what's left of it, is stuck to me like a second skin. I feel half naked. "Lexie? Beth Ann?" I call out. I'm sure they can't hear me. My voice is lost in a whoosh of rain, rustling leaves, and wind. But I can hear them. Their shouts are louder.

I'm getting closer. It's Devin's gravelly voice, all right, but I can't make out all the words. "Come on ... Lexie, no."

Then Lexie's. "Where's mommy when ... need her ..."

"Let's, go, Lex. Before ... comes."

"Precious mommy ... save you now."

I see them.

22

Beth Ann and Devin are shining flashlights at something on the ground, but a headstone is blocking my view. I slow down and walk carefully. I don't call their names. If they hear me, they'll try to get rid of me like the others.

The cloudburst is over now, giving way to a steady patter of soft rain. I can see Devin and Beth Ann clearly, but they haven't noticed me even though I'm only a few yards away. Their open, white robes are streaked with red stains, probably ketchup that washed off in the rain. Under the robes, they're wearing long nightgowns, ripped up and raggy. White paste and clumps of dirt cake their skin and hair. Green goop is leaking out of their eyes. I know it's all fake, but the effect is still terrifying.

Lexie is crouching on the ground, wearing a long, black, hooded cape. The hood casts a dark shadow over her face. She's shouting at something that looks like a pile of clothes. "You and your ugly mother didn't really think we'd initiate you, did you?"

Devin pulls on Lexie's arm. "Lexie, come on. I'm soaking wet. We're going to get sick."

Lexie shakes her off without glancing back. "Where's your precious mommy now, huh?" Then she makes the strangest sound, a kind of animal noise, like a deep growl. It builds into a scream, so forceful I think it's going to lift her off her feet. If rage were a sound, this would be it. She pounds her fists into whatever's behind the headstone, until Beth Ann and Devin grab her arms and hoist her up.

"Let go of me!" Lexie screams.

"Lexie." They all turn at the sound of my voice. It rings out loud and clear because the rain has just stopped. Their flashlights blind me.

"Get out of here, Peyton," Beth Ann warns as I walk toward them. "Cemetery Night's over now. Go home."

"Where's Ellika?" I ask, knowing the answer already, knowing she's the thing behind the headstone. The instant the words come out of my mouth, I see her. Two axes are planted next to her head, blades deep in the mud, handles up.

Ellika is lying face up in the grass, next to her overnight bag, with her sleeping bag tangled in a pile over her legs. Her eyes are closed, but she can't be sleeping. Something is wrong. Very wrong. She's not moving.

"What happened to her?" I ask. No one answers.

They look at Lexie, who says nothing. "Lexie, what happened to her?" I ask. She still doesn't say anything. "Tell me." Lexie is standing right in front of me, but she's not seeing me. She's watching something inside her head.

Beth Ann steps in front of her. "Nothing happened. Smellika's probably faking." She carefully nudges Ellika with her foot, the way you check the pool water to make sure it's not too cold, and pulls one of the axes out of the ground. The blade comes dangerously close to Ellika's face. "I'm out of here. You okay now, Lex?"

Lexie rubs her temples, squeezing her eyes shut. "Yeah, I'm okay," she answers with Zen calm, as if she wasn't completely off her hinges a minute ago. "Smellika and her mommy dearest just make me so sick. Guess I got a little carried away." What a lie. Lexie was more than just a little carried away. I saw enough to know she snapped a vital reality cord.

But she's focused now, in control. "Don't forget the other axe, Beth Ann. Peyton, you get the flashlights."

"You can't just leave her here," I say. "She's out cold."

"Someone will find her in the morning," Beth Ann says, pulling the second axe out of the mud. "We need to get out of here before someone sees us." She sees my hesitation. "If you're worried she's going to tell, forget it."

"Right," says Lexie. "If she hasn't narced on us yet, she'll shut up about this too. Besides, she's probably not even sure who's who. Look at you guys." Devin and Beth Ann look down at themselves, proud of their grisly get-ups.

"We'll say it was two JV girls," says Devin. They start walking away. They don't look back at Ellika.

"I'm not leaving her here." They stop, surprised I'm not right behind them.

"Oh, yeah?" Devin says. "What are you going to do with her? Take her home? Have a sleepover?"

"Look at her!" I shout. Can't they see? She's wet, she's unconscious, she doesn't look right. Something is seriously wrong. "We need to call her parents."

"Call her parents? Are you insane?" Beth Ann yells.

"Shut up, Beth Ann." Lexie's teeth are clenched. "We've already made enough noise. Let's bail, already, before someone hears us and we get arrested for trespassing."

"If we do, it's because you were screaming like a psycho," Beth Ann snaps.

"I'm warning you." Lexie takes a step toward Beth Ann. Her fists are balled up. Is she going to hit her? "You're pissing me off."

"We should take her to the emergency room," I say. "What if she has a concussion?"

Lexie laughs at me. "You need to go on a drama-free diet, Prairie Girl. She just blacked out because we scared the crap out of her. There's no concussion. It's not like she was in a car accident, for chrissakes."

"Can we go now?" Devin whines. "We'll all catch cold if we don't get dry."

I'm not going anywhere. "We can't leave her."

"She freaked out, fainted, and fell," Lexie says. "She'll wake up with a few bruises and call a cab or something.

And *voila,* she'll go home and forget about cheering and never bother us again."

"We can't leave her."

"Peyton, I don't know what's gotten into you, but if you know what's good for you, you'll come with us." I stare down at Ellika. This would never have happened if I'd told her what she needed to know a few hours ago. I could have prevented this. I never even told her I was sorry for all the things we did.

The things I did.

"No."

"I mean it, Peyton."

"So do I."

Lexie lets out a slow, exhausted sigh. "Look, I know what she looks like right now, but don't be weak. Do yourself a favor. Don't go around feeling sorry for people just because they're losers. Leave that to the Smellikas of the world."

I'm not weak. In fact, right now, I feel stronger than I've felt in a long time, stronger than I've ever felt in my whole life.

"I'm not leaving."

Lexie slips her hood off, pushing her face into mine. "Oh yes, you are. Use your head. You'll jeopardize the whole squad. Now come on. We're getting out of here. Move." She doesn't look like herself at all. Her eyes are muddy pools with dark circles underneath. The rain destroyed every fluff of her baby-soft hair, and her skin looks sickly pale. She looks every bit as ghostly as Beth Ann and Devin.

She gives my arm a tug. "I said, move. Now."

"No." I don't have to be a bitch to get what I want. That's not me—and what I want, more than anything at this moment, is to be me again. The me I used to know, the me that would never leave an unconscious girl in a cemetery all night, no matter who told me to.

She gives me another tug, digging her nails into my arm this time. "Come on."

I fling her hand off of me. It's time for my rebel yell. "NO!"

"What the—"

"I'm not going anywhere with you."

Her eyes flash. *Excusez moi?*

"You heard me." She's not fooling me anymore. Her glow is gone. Here, in the darkness of the cemetery, I can see her for what she truly is: damaged.

She squints, searching my face. "Think about what you're doing."

"I know exactly what I'm doing." I push my chin up. She does the same. It's a stand-off. Neither one of us moves. Finally, a nod of understanding: I'm not going with her. I'm not in her power anymore. She's lost me.

"Big mistake, Prairie Girl." She shakes her head like I'm a lost cause. Then she takes off, catching up with the other two. Their robes fly out behind them like dragon wings.

23

It's pouring again. I'm running. Just a few more blocks and I'll be home.

I left the flashlight on, so the ambulance people found her pretty fast. They didn't see me behind the trees, watching. I panicked when I saw the flashing lights. I didn't want them asking any questions about how this happened or who I am. But I stayed and watched them load her onto the stretcher and cover her with a blanket.

It all runs through my head like a film. Trying to make her open her eyes: "Ellika, can you hear me?" Feeling around the inside of her bag for her cell phone, finding it in her sleeping bag, realizing there's blood on my hand and on the phone, unzipping it and pulling back the cover, my hands trembling, so scared, so scared, the gash on her calf, her leg twisted at that angle, going in the wrong direction, the panic, the panic... calling 9-1-1, telling them my name was Ellika Garret, dashing away when I saw the ambulance lights coming up the street.

Mom is waiting up for me. My teeth are chattering. She wants answers. I slam the bathroom door. Take a hot shower. She's waiting with tea. I have to deal with her.

"Next time, call me. You know I'll always come and get you, right?"

"Yeah."

"Was it Von?"

"Yeah."

"That's why you ran home in the rain? Alone, at this hour?"

"Yeah."

"Did he try to go too far, Junebug?"

"Yeah."

"Then you did the right thing."

~ ~ ~

I want to know what happened to Smellika, but I'm too afraid to call the hospital. Does the hospital have caller ID?

I barely slept last night. I feel like death warmed over— sore throat, cough, watery eyes. Even so, I'd welcome pneumonia if I could get out of going to school tomorrow.

I can't get out of it, though. I have to go. Coach Wisser called and said, "It's imperative that both JV and varsity attend school tomorrow. Dr. Johnson wants to see all of us first period." Weird that she said "us" instead of "you."

The show's over. We're in for it. That's what's really making me sick, not this hellish head cold. I call Carmen and Marisol, but just get their voicemail. They don't call me back. Same thing with Sloane. No emails either.

I wish I knew what was happening tomorrow with this meeting, and what happened to Smellika. I'm sure there's at least one person who knows.

But I can't call Lexie anymore.

~ ~ ~

It's tense. Everyone here is prepping themselves for Dr. Johnson. I'm steeling myself for another face-off with Lexie. So far she's kept her back to me. She's giving me the cold shoulder, sitting in the only chair that has a cushion, picking at her nails and looking fashionably bored.

Coach Wisser has been in his office for a half hour. JV was only in there for ten minutes. No one was crying when they came out. That's a good sign.

My joints ache. I feel feverish. This cold is turning into the flu. No one is looking at me. But then again, no one is looking at anybody. We're all too busy rehearsing our defense, how we're going to talk our way out of getting suspended. I'm more concerned about losing my scholarship.

I'll just tell them I wasn't involved. I didn't plan Cemetery Night. I wasn't even there until after it was over. Mr. Pappas will vouch for me, say I'm a good kid, trying hard. Then I'll beg them not to call Mom. I'll crawl on my hands and knees if I have to.

Coach Wisser swings the door open. "You can't pin this on me, Stan. I didn't know anything about it."

Dr. Johnson's voice is dry. "I find that hard to believe."

"So do I." That sounds like Ms. Finch, our phantom vice-principal who rarely makes an appearance. Maya and I used to call her Ms. Pinch, because she makes these faces like someone is pinching her.

Coach Wisser lets go of the door handle. "You'll be hearing from my attorney." By the time the door clicks shut, she's already out of the waiting room.

Lexie springs to her feet. "Wait, Coach Wisser! Laura!" But our once-beloved coach is gone, down the hall and out of sight, without a glance back at Lexie or any of us.

She knew. She knew the whole time. And she did nothing.

"Do you think she got fired?" Pinkie asks. No one has a chance to tell her it sure looks that way, because Dr. Johnson buzzes his secretary to let us in.

"Let me do all the talking," Lexie says before leading us into his big office. There's a semicircle of mini-couches and chairs where Mr. Pappas and Ms. Finch are sitting. I transmit Mr. Pappas a telepathic message: *I'm innocent, I'm innocent!*

Dr. Johnson is sitting behind his desk, glaring down at us. I guess when you're a short man in charge of kids who tower over you all day, it's a good feeling to look down at the suckers you're about to suspend. Like us, I realize with dread.

He adjusts his polyester tie. "I'm sure you all know you're here because of what happened to Ellika Garret."

"What happened to Ellika?" asks Lexie with honey-dripping sweetness. Her makeup is soft today. "No one's told us anything." She's wearing the sky-blue uniform dress, accessorized with a simple white headband. A diamond cross sparkles at her throat. And is that Love's Baby Soft I smell?

An angel. She's transformed herself into an angel. Her new, calculated image says it all perfectly: Lexie Court is shiny and golden; she is incapable of orchestrating a vicious attack on a fellow student.

But Lexie must have forgotten how little Dr. Johnson cares about image. "You really have no idea, Miz Court." It's a sarcastic statement, not a question. He's pissed. This isn't his usual, dull, I'm-talking-but-I'm-really-asleep style. His new tone throws Lexie off balance. I can see it. She's used to being a snake charmer.

But Dr. Johnson is no snake. He's a smart man in ugly clothes, and he's about to give us our sentence.

"Well then, let me be the first to inform you. Ellika Garret has a fractured leg." Lexie's surprised expression doesn't faze him. "It happened Saturday night, after the dance. Her mother told us of a supposed sleepover with the JV squad. Interestingly, JV knew nothing about it."

"Yes, they did," Lexie says. "I emailed all of them."

"They claim they were not informed."

"They're lying."

Dr. Johnson crosses his arms, studying her. So does Ms. Finch, who sneers and says, "A slumber party in a cemetery, Lexie? Care to explain that one?'

"Certainly. It's an initiation ritual. It builds trust. A

squad has to have a close bond to work together effectively. Ellika didn't go through the usual process the rest of us did, in JV. This was just a way to include her."

Mr. Pappas asks quietly, "So everyone was supposed to sleep at the cemetery?"

"Yes. The idea is, they make it through the night together, then *voila*, they have a bond. It's a beautiful thing, really. Lots of teams have these sorts of activities to create unity. I'm just sorry JV ruined it all by not showing up."

"They claim they never got word of any of this."

Lexie sighs, shakes her head. "They're so irresponsible."

Ms. Finch explodes. "That's the most ridiculous pile of rot I've ever heard. You all deliberately lied to Mrs. Garret and to Ellika so you could harass her."

Lexie clasps her hands over her heart. "That's not true. I dropped her off at the cemetery and drove away. I thought JV was in there waiting for her, I swear."

"Well, someone was waiting for her. Ellika Garret was assaulted."

"Assaulted? By who?" Lexie's shock seems so genuine, she's almost convincing me.

"That's what you're going to tell us," Dr. Johnson says, scanning each one of our faces.

"But how would we know anything?" Lexie asks.

Dr. Johnson goes on as if no one has spoken. "Unfortunately, Ellika couldn't see her assailants very well. They were wearing costumes. She also has problems with her vision and it was dark out, so she couldn't identify who was hounding her." Or she doesn't want to identify them. Ellika is so afraid of Lexie, she won't tell on anybody. "All she said was that there were three assailants, all girls. While she was trying to escape, she fell on a gravestone and fractured her leg."

"She also hit her head in the fall and suffered a minor concussion," Mr. Pappas adds.

Lexie opens her mouth to say something, but Dr. Johnson holds up his hand like a traffic cop before she gets a word out.

"Enough. Don't deny it. I know the varsity squad was involved. JV wasn't there at all, so don't insult my intelligence any more by bringing them into it. My job is to find out who was behind this cruel hoax, and who was responsible for her injury. The guilty parties will be expelled." *Expelled*. He says it again. "Expelled."

The room is starting to spin. Juretha is crying. Pinkie is crying. *Expelled*. I grip the arms of my chair like my life depends on it.

"A full investigation is going to be conducted, and let me assure you, we will be thorough. At this point, all of you face possible expulsion." He waits, relishing the pin-drop quiet.

"Here's the good news," says Ms. Finch. "Ellika's mother has generously offered not to press criminal charges as long as we find and punish the guilty parties accordingly."

Criminal charges? As in jail? The big house? The slammer?

All the blood in my head travels down to my feet.

"We're going to handle this in-house. I advise you all to cooperate to the fullest, unless, of course, you'd rather cooperate with the police. Any one of you, or several of you, I suspect, could face charges of battery and/or intentional infliction of emotional distress and whatever other charges they want to come up with."

"We have nothing to confess," says Lexie.

"Knock it off, Lexie," says Ms. Finch. "You better get your squad to tell us what happened or this is all going to get a lot worse."

Dr. Johnson clears his throat. "Mrs. Garret also brought to our attention that this is not an isolated incident. It pains me to say that there have been numerous indications that Ellika has been harassed by you girls. You'll all be called in individually for questioning."

"That was at her other school," says Lexie. "Her mother is confused."

Dr. Johnson doesn't even turn his head in Lexie's direction. "Your parents will all be notified today of what happened Saturday night and your alleged involvement." *No, no, no!* "I suggest you all check the student handbook section on bullying, before you say you have nothing to confess. As of today, you will not be performing at any games or school functions until further notice. JV will take over your home games."

"That's not fair," says Lexie.

"Oh, I think it's more than fair," says Ms. Finch.

Dr. Johnson smooths down his comb-over. "May I just say, on a personal note, how deeply disappointed I am in all of you. I've known most of you since you were in kindergarten, and I never expected this shameful behavior from any of you."

"But they didn't mean to hurt her so badly."

Did I say that?

Please let it be someone else who just said that.

"What?" Dr. Johnson asks me. He cocks his head, the way a hunting dog does when it hears a noise in the distance. The squad shoots me panic-stricken looks. Except for Lexie. Her eyes are loaded with cool hatred.

"Who didn't mean to hurt her, Peyton?" asks Mr. Pappas in such a gentle, kind way I could almost fall apart and tell him everything.

Almost. I swallow, hearing the saliva crackle over my sore throat. "Whoever did it, I mean. There's no one here who would want Ellika to break her leg. No one would want that." I swallow again. "That's all I meant."

24

Everyone has something to say on the way to our lock-ers. I'm the only one who's speechless.

"This is bullshit. I'm not getting expelled for this."

"He said we're facing the *possibility* of expulsion. It's not a done deal."

"If everyone denies it all, they've got nothing."

I listen, getting my books for next period out of Lexie's locker. I keep my head down, hiding behind my hair.

"Technically, we're not supposed to be questioned without a parent or guardian present. I saw that on *Law & Order*."

"I'm pleading the fifth."

"We're all pleading the fifth, right?"

Only kids who've grown up with money feel this con-fident, this untouchable. They don't see doom coming, like I do. I'm sure I'm the only one who feels like there's a tornado headed our way and I'm about to get sucked in. And what about Ellika? Not one of them has mentioned her since we left Johnson's office. Don't any of them feel bad about her leg?

"Cat got your tongue, Plankton?" says Lexie. Their chattering stops. Who's Plankton?

Slam.

The locker door closes hard on my fingers, bounces back open. Intense, intense pain shoots through my fingers and up my arm. Red spots dance in front of my eyes. I gasp, cradling my hand with the other. My knees buckle. "Why don't you speak up now, Prairie Girl?" Lexie spits out "Prairie Girl." It's not a pet name anymore. "You weren't afraid to talk before, almost getting us all expelled."

This time I'm ready. When she slams the door again, my hands are out of the way. "You planning to turn us in, Plankton?" Her smile is more angelic than ever, peaceful as a sunrise. I back away from her, from all of them. "You do know what Plankton means, don't you? Pond scum. It's another word for scum like you."

I can't stay here. It's dangerous. I have to go home. Now. "Remember the pact." Lexie's voice follows me down the stairwell. "Or else."

~ ~ ~

Mom is home. "What are you doing here?" We both say.

Neither one of us answers. She's cleaning out our Tupperware cabinet. She only does that when she's mad. "Your school just called." She stacks three Tupperware bowls, sets them down with a thud. "Don't you have something to tell me?" I sit down at the kitchen table, close my eyes, wait for her to rip into me, brace myself for it. "You're in big trouble, Missy. Your math teacher called. You have a D+. Do you know what that means? Do you? You could lose your scholarship."

I blink at her, numb. That's what she thinks I have to tell her. Trig is just a bump in the road compared to what's hanging over me now. My face collapses. I cover it with my hands. "And why didn't you tell me you were getting tutored? I have a right to know these things, Peyton. I'm your mother, last time I checked. Peyton? Peyton? Did something else... what's wrong?"

I'm so tired, so tired. Exhausted. It's all been too much, for so long now. It's such a relief to let it all out, from the beginning, from the first day of school, with Ellika bouncing up there on the stage, so excited and waving at us. I tell her every hazing stunt we pulled and everything I did.

She listens. She doesn't say much. She's disappointed in me. I've let her down. I've intentionally hurt another human being. I joined the hanging party. She didn't raise me this way. I know better, she tells me.

I know I know better. And I can't answer her big question: how I could have been a part of something so cruel, why I did it. "I wanted to be popular," sounds so lame, so feeble of an excuse. But then, there is no excuse for what we did to Ellika Garret. "I wanted to be Lexie's friend." It's honest, but it's not much of an answer. It makes me cry.

"Why was Lexie so important to you that you could torture a poor girl like that?"

"Mom, Lexie has this, I don't know, charisma." I sniffle. "But it's more than that. It's like she has this power over people. I can't explain it, but you'd know what I mean if you were around her."

"Peyton, don't you know you should never, ever do anything you know in your heart is wrong? You can talk about Lexie all you want, but you made choices here. You did those things to that poor girl. You."

There are times when Mom is right. This is one of them. I knew that hazing Ellika was hurtful and vicious. I knew, and I did it anyway, to be accepted by Beachwood's elite. And now there's nothing I can do to fix the damage I've caused, nothing I can do to erase this monumental feeling of regret.

"I'm so disappointed in you," she says. I know how she feels. I'm disappointed in me, too.

Mom wants to go to school and explain everything to Dr. Johnson. I get so hysterical, begging her to let me handle it, that she gives in. "I can deal with you getting a suspension, but whatever happens, don't lose your scholarship, Junebug. With a degree from Beachwood you'll get into any college you want. You may not get a scholarship, 'specially with your trig grades, but you'll get in. Then we can get financial aid. What? What is it?"

"These are the Garrets, Mom. Like the Garret Foundation Garrets that are always in the paper. They're expelling us, not suspending us."

A sharp intake of breath. "Expelling?" I nod, wiping my eyes. "You're sure?"

"I'm sure." The horror of my situation grips me and I'm really bawling now. "Oh, God, Mom, what am I going to do?"

Mom starts pacing, something she does when she needs to think. "If you get expelled, it goes on your permanent record. You have to tell Dr. Johnson that Lexie was the mastermind behind it all. Peyton, you have to tell."

"No, no, no, Mom—"

"You are *not* getting expelled. It's the only way to save yourself."

"They'll kill me. The girls on the squad, they really will."

"Then I'm going down there and blowing the whistle myself. That'll fix Lexie's little red wagon." I get hysterical again at this idea. She finally backs down. "You have one week, you hear? After that, if it's not resolved, I walk over to your school and tell them everything." I agree to her terms, but I don't know what I'm going to do.

Lexie's turned against me, the squad hates me, I might get expelled, and I have no friends. It doesn't get any worse than this. I'm standing on the edge of the abyss. My life is being ripped to shreds.

~ ~ ~

According to the Beachwood Preparatory Academy Student Handbook, examples of bullying are: 1) physical abuse, e.g., hitting, kicking, pushing, shoving, slapping, or tripping; 2) stealing or damaging another person's private property; 3) teasing; 4) verbal abuse; 5) touching or showing private body parts; 6) ganging up on someone; 7) harassment, in person or by phone, internet, email, cell phone, or other electronic device.

We are so guilty on every count.

I've been in bed for three days. Mom says I'm healthy enough to go back to school. Rude Office Lady called and Mom told her I'd be back today.

I've been getting phone calls, mostly from Lexie, but I recognize Kaitlyn and Shawntay's voices, too.

"Bitch. You better not say a word, or it'll be the last word you ever say."

"You were the last one there. You broke her leg. That's what everyone is saying."

"Have you checked your email lately?" I haven't. I have a pretty good idea of what kind of emails are waiting for me. I don't think I could take it. I need to stay strong, the way I felt in the cemetery.

At least I remembered it's a no-uniform day. I have my Chip and Pepper jeans on, the ones Lexie and Beth Ann were asking about. That should give me a boost if the going gets rough. Amazing how clothes can do that.

I purposely get to school fifteen minutes late. No need to face Lexie and everyone at the lockers. The first thing I see are my textbooks and notebooks. They're all over the floor of the long hallway, like they were kicked or thrown.

Lexie helps out in the office. She knew I'd be in school today. I dial her combination, but the lock doesn't open. I try again. Same thing. This is a different lock.

I gather up as much of my stuff as I can and go to my old locker. It's full of trash. Someone poured a wastebasket in there. Papers and pencil shavings are everywhere. A sign is hanging from the top shelf: *White Trash Lives Here.* I take a deep breath and brace myself for the rest of the day.

Operation Peyton is in effect.

~ ~ ~

In Pavlich's class, there's a new girl in my seat. She's chubby, with highlighted brown hair and a trendy outfit. Mrs. Pavlich is showing a video on the solar system. The back rows aren't watching it. They're laughing and getting up to look at something on the back bulletin board. They whisper like crazy when they see me.

Mrs. Pavlich takes my hall pass, her eyes still glued to the TV screen. I walk past my seat, straight to the bulletin board. The first paper is a list, titled *Top Ten White Trash Rednecks.* I'm number one. And number two. And three, and four, all the way down to ten.

The next page shows a computer-generated picture of me in my cheerleading uniform, standing next to cows. I'm in a basing stance, but instead of holding up Pinkie or Lexie, my arms are reaching up to hold piles of steaming cow manure. A third paper shows a trailer with the words "Plankton Grady's House" scribbled across it.

Someone snickers. I want to rip them down, but my

arms aren't working. Compular does it for me, crumpling them up into little balls. "Whatsa-matter, can't them rednecks take a joke in West Virgin-ee?" Justin says.

"Forget them," Compular says to me under his breath. "Don't listen." He sits back down, throwing the papers in the trash. He's trying to grow a soul patch. It looks like there's a piece of lint stuck to his chin.

"You're in my seat," I say to the new girl. She has a cast on her leg.

It can't be.

No sideways ponytail. It's styled in layers. Her squished-together eyes blink three times. They keep doing it. Blink, blink, blink. She finally got contact lenses. It is her. She's had the mother of all make-overs. "Ellika, you're in my seat."

"Her name is Elle," Lexie says. "And don't you forget it."

"Yeah." Blink, blink, blink. "From now on, I'm Elle. Right, Lexie?"

"Right." Now Ellika is Elle, and she's got Lexie in her corner. The whole world's gone crazy. Or just my world, anyway. "There's a seat in front of me, Prairie Girl," says Lexie. She's wearing a baby blue tee that says *I Cheer for Jesus* in big bubble letters.

Compular pats the empty desk next to him. I sit there. Last week I wouldn't have dreamed of sitting anywhere near him, but right now, being near Compular makes me feel safe. Dorkowitz is on the other side of me. Lexie flicks the back of Dorkowitz's head and orders him to switch seats with her. He does it without a word.

She slides into his seat, scoots the chair closer to me. "So, Plankton, do you buy all your clothes at Goodwill? Or just my cast-offs?" Her cast-offs? She thinks these jeans are hers.

"Did I hear a question, dear?" warbles Mrs. Pavlich.

"No, thank you, Mrs. Pavlich. I know the answer to my question," Lexie says.

"I don't buy my clothes at Goodwill," I say. It sounds like a lie, even to my own ears.

"Well, that's pretty interesting, because those jeans are Lexie's throw-aways," says Beth Ann. "I'd recognize them anywhere. Remember when your maid sewed on those tacky appliqués and ruined them, Lex? Not even the other maids would take them for a hand-me-down." A hundred red-hot needles are pricking me all over, burning me with humiliation. My embarrassment is unbearable. I close my eyes.

"Yup, that's right," says Lexie. "The genius thought she'd surprise me and she got fired instead. But that's okay. They made good charity jeans, obviously. They're trailer fabulous. Goodwill's always happy to take old clothes for po' folks like ya'll, ain't that right, Plankton?" Everything is swirling around me again, like I'm at the center of a whirlpool. It's that tornado I was worried about. It's happening. I'm getting sucked in.

"Plankton," Beth Ann calls to me. "Did you know Chip and Pepper jeans have special names for each style? That style is called Walk of Shame. Did you hear me? Walk of Shame. It was 'in,' like, a million years ago."

"Walk of shame," Lexie repeats. "How appropriate."

They see it on me, my shame. They've probably always seen it. It's all I can feel. Hot, scalding shame.

Elle forces out these big, phony, nasal laughs. Lexie winces, but gives Elle a stiff smile. "Bloomie's, my ass. Where's your shirt from, Plankton, the Salvation Army? You can't even afford to be at this school, you welfare case."

"She's always been a poseur, trying to pass herself off as one of us," says Beth Ann. A heavy weight is pressing down on my chest. I can't breathe.

"Shut up, both of you," says Compular.

"Ooh, are you her new boyfriend?" Lexie asks him.

"Jeez, Lexie, what's your Native American name, Dripping Venom?" he says. "You don't even know what you're talking about. You're so full of it, Lexie."

"Ssshhh," says Kim Wu. She's watching the video and taking notes.

"You're the one who's full of it, Compular," Hunter says. "Why don't you tell us another one of your bullshit stories, you douche."

"Why don't you make us lose another game, you useless jockstrap," he fires back. Hunter gets out of his seat, fists clenched, jaw pumping.

"Sit down, *mon amour*," Lexie says to Hunter. "Let's not change the subject." He sits down, giving Compular the finger. "Beth Ann, have you seen the crapshack she lives in? Sloane, have you seen it? No? Well, you should." Sloane lifts her head out of her magazine and looks at me with pity. Someone feeling sorry for me is almost as bad as someone being mean to me. Ellika won't look at me at all. "I didn't know people could live like that. And you should see her mother, too."

"No, in West Virgin-ee, they say momma," says Justin.

"Is her hair as red as her neck?" Hunter asks.

"You know what? It is," Lexie laughs. They high five each other.

The tornado stops. Lexie is crossing the line, making fun of my mother. Something shifts inside me, releasing the weight on my chest. The needles aren't pricking me anymore. My mother has more class than all of these people combined. How dare they degrade her? Who are they to put me down and try to make me feel so worthless?

I look around at all of them. It's a revelation, like the first time I could recognize words and read when I was little and it made the whole world look different. For three years, I've been working toward their acceptance, aching to be one of them. But I couldn't read what was right in front of me. They're not out of my league. I'm out of theirs.

I'm nothing like them. They may have thought hazing Ellika was a necessary measure, and maybe even had fun doing it, but I knew better from day one. It was wrong. It ate me up inside. Yet I took part in all of it, doing every heinous thing I was told to do, all to be an Alpha. I was so dazzled by Lexie, I couldn't see what Maya saw all along. I was never Alpha material. I was never a shark.

I was something better.

"You're the last person who should be talking about anyone's mother," I say.

A hardness flickers over Lexie's face. "Shut your hole, Peyton."

"Your mother's a train wreck compared to mine. Compared to anybody's."

She sits up suddenly, like a marionette being yanked by a string. "I said shut up."

Fear is written all over her. She's afraid I'll tell, afraid I'll broadcast her secrets the way she's broadcast mine. Well, she can be as afraid as she wants. As for me, I'm tired of being afraid. And I'm tired of feeling ashamed. Lexie Court has more reason to feel fear and shame than me. Way more.

I stand up. "You don't scare me, Lexie."

Someone is clapping. It's Compular. His look of admiration fills me up.

"Where are you going?" asks Mrs. Pavlich as I walk out.

"Kmart must have a blue-light special," Justin calls out.

I answer him with all the dignity I have. "No. I'm going to Dr. Johnson's office." Mom is right. Telling on Lexie and the others is the only way to save myself. It's eat or be eaten. It's me or them.

25

Dr. Johnson is trying to get in the spirit of dress-down day, wearing a *Save the Whales* T-shirt. "I'm afraid all the evidence points to you, Miss Grady."

"What evidence?"

"This Operation Smellika list, for one thing."

"But, Dr. Johnson, I just told you that was Lexie's. It's in her handwriting."

"The one I have here is typed. But besides that, the girls on the squad say you are responsible for this hazing campaign on Ellika Garret. I've questioned them for the last three days. They all say the same thing."

"And what's that?"

"That you were the brain behind it all. I must say I was shocked to hear their accounts, Miss Grady. I've never known you to be malicious."

"Exactly. I'm not malicious. Why would I have it out

for Ellika Garret? I don't even know her that well. Lexie was the brain behind it, not me."

"It's your word against theirs. The other girls suggested that perhaps your motivation was jealousy."

"Jealous? Me? Of her?"

"In the financial sense, yes."

Oh. Of course. Poor little Peyton, mad at the rich girl. "You said you interviewed the whole squad?"

"Yes."

So Carmen and Marisol, Pinkie and Sloane, they all stabbed me in the back. Some friends. Lexie must have coached everybody with what to say. "What about Elle?"

"Who?"

"Ellika."

"We questioned her, too."

"And she never mentioned Lexie doing anything to her? Or Beth Ann, or Devin?"

"No."

I see where this is going. Lexie made a deal with Ellika: my head on a platter in exchange for membership in the Alphas. And she jumped at the chance.

Dr. Johnson shuffles some papers around on his desk, holds one up and reads it. "Let's see what my notes say. She says you stepped on her glasses. I suppose you're going to tell me that was an accident."

"No. Lexie told me to do it."

"Really? If she told you to jump off a bridge, would you?"

"This was different. She—"

"Ellika Garret is legally blind."

I look down at my lap. "I know."

"And you stepped on her glasses, knowing that?"

It takes me a while to answer. "Yes," I say, feeling like the lowest of the low. "Lexie wanted me to do it. The others did too. So I did it."

"Miss Garret says you stole her uniform before the pep rally."

"Yes, because—"

"Let me guess. Lexie made you do it."

"She did. She—"

"You pushed her down the stairs and ripped her skort."

"I never did that. Lexie did." A heaviness is falling over me. He's burying me, one layer at a time.

"According to Ellika, Lexie helped her up after she'd fallen and asked if she was okay. You, on the other hand, were standing at the top of the staircase, gloating."

"I wasn't gloating. I didn't even push her."

"Your locker is next to hers. You took advantage of that. You hung up those obscene undergarments."

"No. I never did that."

"She says she knows you did it because when you saw her coming, you ran down the stairs."

"I ran down the stairs, yes, because I...I don't know why. But I never put that underwear there. I wouldn't even know where to buy a thing like that."

"Says here you planted the ant colony in her locker."

"Mike and A.J. and Von did that. It was Mike's colony."

"Oh, so now there were boys who wanted her off the cheerleading squad, too, eh?"

I'm drowning, falling fast. I babble, scrambling to keep

my head above water, clawing my way out of this trap. "They wanted to help Lexie. It's true. Dr. Johnson, please believe me. Operation Smellika was all Lexie's plan. She wanted Ellika off the squad. We all did, but especially Lexie. Hunter and Justin thought up Cemetery Night. They'd done it before, with that kid on their football team."

"Your teammates all assume you broke Ellika's leg."

"No, they know I didn't. Beth Ann, Lexie, and Devin. They were the ones chasing Ellika when she fell down and broke it. She passed out and they didn't even check to see if she was okay. I did that."

"Beth Ann and Devin, you say? They left her unconscious?"

"Yes, and Lexie too. They planned it all."

"These are serious allegations, Peyton. Punishable by expulsion at the very least. Do you have proof of all this?"

"Proof? Like how?"

"Tangible evidence. Documents, photos, testimony from one of the other girls who witnessed anything."

"No. But it's all true, I swear it."

"It's your word against theirs."

"Please, Dr. Johnson. I'm sorry for any pain I caused Ellika. I truly am, and I'm willing to take responsibility for my actions. But I'm begging you. Let me prove that Lexie Court is the person you need to expel, not me."

He leans back in his chair, thinking. "I don't know exactly why, Peyton, but I believe you. My instincts tell me you're telling the truth." I slump down with relief. "Still, you say you're willing to take some responsibility."

"I am."

"But I'll still have to punish you. There will be consequences."

"I know."

"You're aware your scholarship is in jeopardy due to a recent drop in your GPA."

"I'm working hard on that, getting tutored. I'll pull it up." My voice gets dry and quivery. "I'll do anything to stay here, sir. I need to graduate with a Beachwood diploma to get into a good college." *And it's all I've ever known.*

He sighs, long and slow. "I can't get you out of this mess without some kind of solid proof that Lexie was the engine behind the machine, and that Beth Ann and Devin were also involved. Without it, I'll have no choice but to expel you. You have until Monday to come up with it."

"But today's only Friday."

"That's correct. It appears you'll need to grow a spine by then, Miss Grady."

~ ~ ~

"Peyton Grady to the science lab immediately." That can't be right. I don't take physics until next semester. But it's Rude Office Lady and she sounds official.

It's eighth period, the end of the day. The lab is empty. Also not right. The head of the science department, Mr. Rathburn, resembles a human/rat hybrid and doesn't often venture out of the lab to mix with regular life forms. "Hello?" I call. My senses are on high alert. "Mr. Rathburn?" The closet door is open. It's right near the main door. "Hello?"

No one is in here. Something is definitely off. I turn to leave. I'm not going near the closet. This is a set-up.

I'm not fast enough. A hard shove and I'm on the floor, getting blindfolded. There's more than one person dragging me. They pull my hair, slap me hard when I start to scream. It all happens so fast I don't even have time to make any noise. A door shuts and locks. "Have fun with the dead baby," Lexie sings from the other side of the door.

"Yeah, and if you get hungry, you can always eat some worms or frogs," says Devin. Their footsteps fade away. Did I hear Juretha laughing?

I pull the blindfold off and rub my cheek. I'll have a bruise there. A few tears roll slowly down my face, like sap from a tree. It seems like the whole universe is against me. My life is unraveling so fast. I thought I had everything. I never thought this would happen to me.

It smells putrid in here, like formaldehyde and mold. There's a sheet of light coming in under the door, but other than that, it's pitch dark. I stand up and feel around for the light switch, petrified of what I might touch by accident. What if live worms escaped? Or mice? I think I heard a story that someone got locked in here twenty years ago over winter break and died.

I find the light switch, flick the lights on. I think I want to turn them back off. Display cases of insects are on the shelf closest to me. A full-size skeleton stands in the corner. A refrigerator hums in the back.

There it is. The dead baby, floating in a jar of filmy white fluid. I yelp and cover my mouth. Its eyes look plastic. Hey, wait, they are plastic. I take a closer look. Totally plastic. This is no dead baby. This is a doll.

I can't believe it. The whole school is terrified of the science closet, and all that's in it is a doll and a few dead bugs. There are no dead monkeys or human body parts here. It feels good to smile. There's a terrarium next to the doll with a giant plastic spider inside, the creepy kind they show on the National Geographic channel. I could plant that in Lexie's backpack. I lift up the lid and reach in to take the spider out.

And then I scream bloody murder.

It's hairy. And moving. The baby may be fake, but the huge spider is very real. My hand jerks out, knocking over a stack of magazines behind the terrarium. Somehow I manage to click the lid down tight. I scoop up the magazines, backing as far away from the spider as possible. It isn't until the magazines are all in a nice, neat pile that I realize what they are.

Naked ladies. This is serious perv material. There must be fifty nudie mags here. I flip through a few. I have to look. There's no one here but me.

Now my scholarship is really worth something, because I'm getting a whole new education from these pictures. Coach Wisser should have used these for sex ed instead of those dumb diagrams.

Except for the live, hairy spider, the horror stories about the science supply closet must be myths. And I know why. Mr. Rathburn started all the rumors himself to keep kids from finding his private stash. I open up a centerfold.

Which sparks a great idea. Now I know how I can get proof.

26

I'm only locked in for a half hour before Mr. Rathburn hears me knocking. He doesn't even ask how I got locked in or do I have a pass or anything. What a weirdo. He just looks behind the terrarium and makes like he's talking to the spider. "Poor Charlotte, did she wake you?" It's so obvious that what he's really doing is checking to make sure his porn supply is still intact.

The *Beacon* office is busy, just like I thought. Sloane is here, ignoring me and working on her column. I'm sure it'll all be lies about me. Jamar says Maya went home early. Something is up with that. She would never leave early on a deadline day without a good reason. I'm not here to see her, though.

The guy I need to see is bending over the light table, viewing negatives through a loop lens. I have to stop myself from calling him Compular. "Ryan."

His grin feels like a hug. "Hi." He glances at Sloane.

"How're you doing? Your cheek is all red. Are you okay?" he whispers.

"Hanging in there," I whisper back. "I need your help." I toss my head toward Sloane. "Not here." We go to the photography lab. "I need a favor. You're always taking pictures. Do you save all of them?"

"Yeah, they're on disc."

"Could I look at them?"

"Sure. Why?"

"Let me look first. Then I'll explain."

We don't find the ammunition I was hoping for. It's such a letdown. If only he'd gotten more shots of what I need. The only picture that's useful to me is one of Lexie hanging the granny panties above Ellika's locker.

"That was early in the morning, before school started," he explains. We're sharing a chair at the computer. "I was doing my community service hours, helping Mr. Pappas with his computer, and I caught her right in the act."

"Did she see you?"

"No. I'm a good spy."

"Really? You don't look like one."

"Sure I do. The name's Bond. James Bond."

He has a candid picture of Kim Wu handing out flyers in the hallway. In the background, there's a clear view of Beth Ann and Devin shoving Ellika's face in the water fountain. I could use this one. We could blow it up and crop it. There aren't any of Cemetery Night because he wasn't there, but these are a start for the proof Dr. Johnson needs. It's not enough, though.

"I'm not proud of these," I say. There are a few shots of Juretha and me dancing at a game, and Ellika is bent in the other direction, doing something totally different. Juretha and I are looking over at her, laughing. My face looks grotesque. I look like a stranger to myself, someone I don't like. Ryan might think less of me looking at these, but not lesser than I think of myself. "We taught her the wrong dance moves on purpose, so she wouldn't be doing what the rest of us were doing. We made her do these really ridiculous retro disco moves."

"I remember."

"It seemed funny at the time."

"You're not laughing now."

"No." I click on another photo. "Hey, that's a good one." There's a picture of me on the sidewalk. "You caught me walking home after school."

"You're the only one I know without a car. Is it hard being on scholarship?"

I stiffen. Lexie may have blown the door wide open on my personal history in Pavlich's class, but it's still none of his business. "I don't talk about that. Besides, what does that have to do with any of this?"

"Sorry, my mouth's an early riser, but my brain sleeps in."

"It's okay. I wish it didn't bother me so much. To talk about it, I mean."

"You shouldn't let it. If you're ashamed of yourself, everyone else will be too."

He's right. I'll have to remember that one. "You are very wise, James Bond. Is it hard when they call you Compular?"

"No, not at all."

"Oh, come on. They don't believe anything you say." No need to reveal that I don't believe him either.

"So? I know I'm not a liar. Why should I care what a bunch of sub-anthropoid halfwits think?"

"Wow. You're going to get really high scores on your SAT verbal."

"I know. But seriously, hear what I'm saying. There's a lot of freedom in not caring what other people think."

Another pearl of wisdom to remember. "I wish I'd figured that one out before Pavlich's class today."

"Forget about those cocky jock morons. Hey, what do you need these pictures for, anyway?"

"I'll tell you. But first, can you give me a ride to Maya's house?"

"Sure."

27

Ryan hasn't even finished parking the car in front of her house when I jump out and almost fall on my face. There's a moving truck in her driveway. Omigod. Maya can't be moving far away, not now, not when I need her most. Please let her just be moving somewhere close. She's standing on the lawn with her back to me, watching the movers load sofas onto the truck.

"Maya!" I shout. Her head whips around. My natural impulse is to run right up to her, but her stony expression nails my feet to the ground. I'm not welcome here anymore.

"What are you doing here?"

"Maya, you don't have to listen, and I don't blame you if you don't. The thing is, I need your help. But first, I just want to apologize." She crosses her arms, still stone-faced. "I messed up. Totally. I should never have put the squad before our friendship, and you'll always be my best friend, even if you never speak to me again."

A few seconds go by, then her face crumples. "You really hurt me, Pey," she says to the ground. "You acted like I didn't even matter to you anymore."

"You *do* matter. You always mattered. It's just that I was so wrapped up in Lexie and everything..." I throw my hands up in a shrug. "I was so busy trying to be someone I'm not, I didn't realize I was letting go of the best friend I ever had."

"You got that right." Her voice is thick with held-back tears.

"You were right about everything. I should have listened to you."

"Peyton, I don't know if I can ever be friends with you again. Not after the way you treated me."

I press my hands together, pleading with her to accept my apology. "Maya, please. I know I screwed up, but we could go back to the way things were, if you give me a chance."

"Maya!" Her mother calls from inside the house. "Come in here, please."

"I, uh, I gotta go," she says and turns around, trudging slowly up the footpath to the front door.

I have to change her mind. "I didn't realize what a gift it was to have you for a friend until it was too late!" I call out.

The front door clicks shut.

It's an effort to stay standing. Because what I really

want to do is fall on the ground and curl up into a ball. I never outgrew Maya. I only thought that because Lexie suggested it. I believed everything Lexie suggested. Lexie was the Dalai Lama, the goddess of beauty and money I worshiped.

But I can't blame her exclusively for the way things are turning out. I have to be honest about my own stupidity. I flew into Lexie's web without looking back because I wanted to shine in her reflected light, no matter what the cost, no matter who I hurt or how low I had to sink.

So I joined the wrecking team and bulldozed Ellika until she was literally broken. Friendless, misfit Ellika, who just wanted what I wanted, to be a popular varsity cheerleader. And I turned my back on my best friend. Now I'm the friendless misfit, and I might be expelled or lose my scholarship. I'll be sorry about what I've done for the rest of my life. As sorry as I am about losing Maya.

I turn around and see Ryan through my watery eyes, leaning against his car waiting for me. I walk toward him, needing to get out of here before I totally lose it.

A hand on my shoulder stops me. "It's not too late, Pey."

I face her. I'm afraid to say it. "You mean you forgive me?"

She wraps her arms around me. I squeeze her tight, soaking up her warmth. I feel peaceful and weightless, the way I do when I'm floating in a pool. She's back. My long-lost sister is back.

"Oh, Maya-mooch, I've made such huge mistakes." I

pull away from our hug so I can see her face to face. "I don't know how to say I'm sorry."

"You just did." A plane roars overhead. We wait for it to pass. When the sky is finally silent, she says, "I have to tell you something."

"What?"

"Just that I ... uh ... I'm sorry, too. I shouldn't have said you have a chip on your shoulder about being on scholarship and all."

I can't believe *she's* apologizing to *me*. "But you were right. I do obsess about it, about the whole money thing. I'm going to work on that. I swear."

"Well, you were right about me, too. I've got to stop being so hard on everybody, myself included. I'm going to work on not acting like I'm your mother."

The perfectionista admitting she has flaws? This is something new. I don't know what to say, so I just ask, "Is that your shrink's advice?"

"Yeah," she says.

"I knew it!" We both laugh through our tears.

"You know what? The shrink's helped me a lot. Therapy's not such a total waste."

"Really?"

"Really. I've learned a lot about myself."

"Yeah, I've learned a lot about myself lately, too." We're quiet for a moment, letting our words settle in. "You know, I don't think you've ever apologized to me. Not for anything important, anyway."

Maya thinks about it, pursing her lips. "Yeah, that's probably true. Guess I'm going to work on that, too."

"So...maybe we both have stuff to work on?"

Her answer is a slow nod. I reach out and tug on one of her curls, then kind of mess up her hair, signaling we're done analyzing ourselves for the moment. The important thing is that we're friends again. Best friends. Everything will be all right with us. I can feel it. And with Maya back in my life, things don't seem so hopeless. She'll help me with the rest of my idea. I know she will.

"I've missed us," she says.

"Not as much as I've missed us, trust me."

Some men walk by, carrying a couch. Panic hits me. I still don't know where she's moving. "Please tell me you're not moving far."

"Huh? We're not moving at all."

"Then what's all this?" I point to some men carrying a table.

"Don't ask. It's my mother. She's on a feng shui kick. We're replacing our furniture."

"So you're not moving?"

"God, no. Mom just decided our stuff doesn't have the right energy. All this stuff is going to the summer house."

"I didn't know feng shui had anything to do with the type of furniture you have," says Ryan, who just walked up.

Maya gives me a *well, well, well, what's this* look before answering him. "It doesn't. Mom just interprets it that way so she can redecorate." Ryan laughs. "Where's Von?" she asks me.

"Don't know, don't care."

"Another BOM, I knew it." Maya links her arm through mine. "Let's go inside. Magda's baking brownies." Ryan trails behind us. She lowers her voice to a whisper. "What's with Compular?"

"We're, like, friends now." Maya raises one eyebrow. "I'm serious, and his name is Ryan."

We go to Dr. Kaplan's study. Ryan and I plop ourselves on the leather couch. Maya sits behind the antique desk and puts her feet up. "Well, what do you need help with? And by the way, what happened to your cheek?"

"Get comfortable," I say. "I have a lot to tell you guys." I stop to chew on my lower lip. "I'm in trouble." How do I start? How can I admit what I did to Ellika? What will they think?

"It's okay, Pey," says Maya. "We're good again. Whatever it is, I've got your back."

"Same here," says Ryan. "You can count on me, too."

~ ~ ~

Maya says Lexie is a pathological narcissist. She got that from a book her shrink loaned her. She also says she's not surprised I got all caught up in Lexie's games because I have self-esteem issues.

Whatever. We're friends again, and that's what matters. Ryan, Maya and I are going to make next week's issue of the *Beacon* a special one, with an exposé article in it.

We're going to work on it all weekend, and call it a *Special Edition*. Maya wants the headline to read: *Breaking News, A Beachwood Exposé Special Report.* We'll use Ryan's photos to go with the story.

Once Dr. Johnson reads the facts about Cemetery Night and Operation Smellika in print, in his very own school newspaper, he'll have to consider it some kind of proof. If not . . . well, I prefer not to think about the "if not" scenario. This is all I've got. It's got to work, even if it's not much.

Then again, this may not be all I've got. Maya asked me if I revealed any hazing stuff in my drama journal, and when I told her I did, she practically burst open from excitement. "Pey, I can't believe you. Why didn't you think of it? It's the perfect proof."

She's convinced I should give Dr. Johnson my drama journal. I read it over and I don't think I could ever let him read it in this lifetime. It has some very private info in there, about Von's lips and the boob ranking, not exactly the documentation he's looking for. I could cross that stuff out, but then it would look like I'm hiding something, and only guilty people have anything to hide. I explained all this to Maya, but she keeps insisting I have to get over myself and turn it in.

Because I did write a lot about Operation Smellika and Cemetery Night. There are a lot of details about that, including my own involvement. I don't want Dr. Johnson to see that either. Maya says I may not have a choice.

What I'm most worried about is what the squad will

do to me after the Special Edition comes out. Maya and Ryan both agree that I should never be alone on campus. They're going to take me home and pick me up every day. I get weak when I think about it.

~ ~ ~

Saturday morning, I race over to Maya's house to get started on our article. I've barely set foot in her bedroom when she hands me some papers. "You're not going to believe this."

"What?"

"Sit down. It's Sloane's column. She emailed it to me."

"I'm afraid to look," I tell her, starting to read.

> *Today your favorite shark is revealing a huge secret, and this isn't a secret about your favorite couple, or who was caught cheating. This is a dark secret, kept hidden from Beachwood students since the year began. It's about an evil plot using the lowest, most depraved methods of hazing, all to kick Ellika Garret off the varsity cheerleading squad. This bullying plan, called Operation Smellika, resulted in Ellika's fractured leg and her new identity as Elle, as well as the shut-down of the varsity cheerleading squad for this year and the termination of Coach Wisser.*
>
> *So who thought up Operation Smellika, you ask? Why, none other than the captain of Beachwood A-Listers herself, Lexie Court, with her band*

of peppy cheerleaders carrying out the hazing orders.

I sit down on Maya's bed and read the rest. She names names. She shows the Operation Smellika list. Sloane wrote about everything, including her own involvement in all the pranks and the pressure to keep the hazing a secret. She uses the word "conspiracy." Mostly, her column features Lexie—all the things she said and did, and also how she turned the tables, blaming everything on me. In one paragraph, she calls Lexie the Hitler Barbie.

I'm stunned. Sloane has exposed herself as one of the hazers, and betrayed Lexie and the whole squad. She's hanging herself with this. I can't understand it.

"Why'd she do it?" Maya asks when I'm finished reading.

"I don't know. She's mental. Or suicidal. They're going to kill her. There has to be some reason why she did this."

Maya leans close to me. "Pey, this is testimony from another witness. And it's a document. Plus, it's exactly what we need for our *Special Edition*. More importantly, it's what *you* need. Sloane may have just saved your butt, girlfriend."

28

"Hello?"

"Sloane?"

"Yes?"

"It's Peyton."

"You've seen my column."

"Yeah." I pause. "Thank you."

"Don't thank me yet. I haven't talked to Dr. Johnson. Or shown him my emails."

"What emails?"

"I printed out every email from Lexie. Even the one detailing our jobs for Cemetery Night."

I drop the phone, pick it back up. "Sloane, that's perfect. That's the proof I need."

"I thought so."

"But why are you doing this? She'll turn on you, too."

"No, she won't. Her days as our captain are over. We don't have a squad anymore, remember?"

"But why now? You went along with everything, like I did."

"Yeah, but it wasn't right. Besides, she—" Sloane stops.

"What?"

Long pause. "She tried to get with Diego at Sadie's. Said they could be friends with benefits, that me and Hunter would never find out. It happened when I was waiting in line for popcorn. I don't know where Hunter was."

So that's the whole reason she wrote the article. Forget about what's right or wrong. It's all about Diego. "That wasn't in your column."

"Diego wanted me to put it in. I told him I don't need people wondering if he cheated on me. Which, of course, he didn't."

"No, of course not."

"You know, Peyton, the best person to expose Lexie and her axis of evil is our haze-ee."

"Haze-ee?"

"Smellika. Ellika. Elle. Whatever her name is these days. That's who you need. I'll tell Johnson to interrogate her again. There's no way she didn't recognize them in the cemetery. I don't care what her eyesight is. She'd have to be headless not to figure it out."

~ ~ ~

It's five minutes until the first-period bell, and already everyone's got a copy. An eerie quiet hangs in the halls.

Kids are reading it and walking slowly, like zombies. Some of them give me nasty looks, some just stare curiously.

Ryan, Maya, and I stop by the principal's office to personally deliver a copy to Dr. Johnson. His secretary takes it, but says he already has one. I hand her my journal, too. Maya's right. It's the best proof I have. And what's one more humiliation, after what Lexie put me through? I've thought about it and decided that humiliation is just part of the price I have to pay for the mistakes I've made. It sucks, but that's the way it is.

Ellika is sitting in the waiting area. Her glasses are back, but her new, highlighted hair is held back with a white headband, similar to the one Lexie wore in Dr. Johnson's office. She's reading the *Special Edition*.

"I just wanted to tell you I'm sorry," I say to her. She doesn't answer. I understand. I know what it's like when Lexie's ordered you not to speak to someone. I wonder if she'll ever learn what I've learned: that you can't pretend to be someone you're not. In the end, the real you will catch up to the fake you.

The door to Dr. Johnson's office opens, and, to my surprise, Mrs. Garret pokes her head out. "Ellika, come in, please. Dr. Johnson needs to speak to you." Ellika stands up.

"I'm sorry about everything," I tell her. Ellika looks like she's going to say something to me, but thinks better of it and just nods instead. Her mother looks at me like a turd has spoken. I'm still glad I said it.

The two-minute-warning bell sounds. Ryan and Maya

walk me to Mrs. Mandolini's room. I haven't seen the squad anywhere. They must all be holed up somewhere, reading it together and planning their next move. The only Alpha I see is Hunter, leaning against the wall, reading.

Dorkowitz makes the mistake of bumping right into him. He was walking and reading the *Special Edition* like everyone else.

"Watch it, Dorkowitz," Hunter snarls without taking his eyes off the paper.

Dorkowitz just stands there. His paper swishes to the floor. "What did you call me?"

Hunter looks down at him and steps away from the wall. "I didn't call you anything. But I'd be happy to call you a geeky little needle-dick, if you like."

Dorkowitz takes a step toward Hunter. Then another one. He looks up at him, chinless face all red, nostrils flaring. "What?" Has Dorkowitz completely lost his brain cells? Hunter will grind him into hamburger meat. *Run, Dorkowitz, run!*

Hunter pushes him. "You heard me." Hunter pushes him again. "Get outta my face, buttcrack."

Dorkowitz doesn't budge.

A few kids passing them slow down, including us. Griffin stops altogether and shouts, "Fight! Fight! Fight!" In the distance, I can see a teacher charging toward us. But it's too late.

"Haaaaaa-yaaahhh!" Dorkowitz yells. His hands and legs fly out in a series of chops and kicks straight out of a

Jackie Chan movie. It's impressive. But not as impressive as seeing Hunter five seconds later on his knees, holding his crotch, with a face twisted in pain.

"My name is David," the karate kid says before walking proudly away in his farting sneakers.

Griffin looks down at Hunter. "Doo-hooode," he laughs. "Looks like you just got dork-spanked."

29

"Well, Miss Grady, I've spoken to Sloane, and I've read the emails and this illustrious publication." He lifts up the *Special Edition Beacon*. "I also read your journal. It was very informative." My face reddens. "You provided a great deal of documentation in a short time."

I gulp, waiting to hear my verdict. My eyebrow is twitching like crazy.

"Nevertheless, it all paled in comparison to when Ellika told me the truth about what happened in the cemetery. You can stop worrying. You're not going to be expelled, Peyton."

I fight back tears of relief, but I lose the battle. He hands me a tissue, and I give him my most heartfelt smile. He smiles back.

I never took a good look at his face before. He happens to have a kind one. I don't think it's true that the eyes are the windows to the soul. I think it's the whole face.

Faces change, and you can see a lot in a person's face, if you pay attention. I know I'll never see the simple beauty I once saw in Lexie's features without seeing the layers of pain and ugliness, too.

Right now, it's Dr. Johnson's pasty face that looks beautiful to me. "Thank you, Dr. Johnson. Thank you so much."

"The bad news is..." *please, not my scholarship* "...that you will be suspended for three days. And you will be banned from athletics for the rest of the year. You and the rest of your squad, those who haven't been expelled, will take a mandatory, after-school sensitivity course in character education, taught by Mr. Pappas. The course runs for a full semester. I sincerely hope you'll use better judgment in the future."

"I will." He hasn't mentioned my scholarship.

"And one more thing."

"Yes?"

"You will remain on scholarship as long as you keep your promise to Mr. Pappas and raise your GPA. I guarantee it." I'm overwhelmed. It's over. It's finally over. I've got my life back. My real life.

Heroes don't always wear tights and a cape. Or a suit of shining armor. Or even the latest "in" brand of designer jeans.

Sometimes heroes just wear really old bell-bottom pants.

30

Lexie and Beth Ann and Devin got expelled. Everyone else on the squad got more or less what I did. Hunter and Justin only got suspended for one day, which is supremely wrong, but not as wrong as Von and his friends getting off scot-free because no one saw them plant the ant colony.

Today's my last day of suspension, and Mom said I could go to the mall with her to watch her do makeup on people. Beth Ann is in the store buying a whole new wardrobe. I've been watching her from behind the makeup counter. There's a saleswoman holding a pile of clothes, following her.

She sees me. Mom is at the other end of the counter, helping a customer. Beth Ann says something to the saleswoman and comes over to me.

She starts trying on eye shadows from the sampler pallet. I arrange the lipsticks in alphabetical order to look like I'm doing something important. I'm not going to say anything first. After a few minutes, she looks in the mirror and says, "Devin and I are going to Palm Glades Prep, in case you're wondering. No uniforms there."

"Good for you." If I was smart, the conversation would end here. But I have to know. "Where's Lexie going?"

Her eyes meet mine. "You mean you haven't heard?"

"Heard what?"

"You really don't know."

"Know what?"

"Lexie's in Zurich."

I must not have heard her correctly. "Where?"

"Switzerland, *duh*. Some boarding school."

We should have sent that little bitch to Swiss finishing school years ago. Lexie's gone? Just like that? Beth Ann must be messing with me.

"She never even said good-bye to Hunter. Just got on the plane and left"—Beth Ann snaps her fingers—"like that."

What?

Lexie is gone. It sounds impossible, but I know she's telling the truth. Lexie is out of our orbit, out of our lives. This information takes a while for me to grasp. I may never see her again. She's out of here. For good. It's too hard to comprehend. Lexie has been the engine driving us for so long.

I was prepared for her to be expelled, but not erased. She's like a celebrity. I assumed there'd be Lexie sightings around town from time to time. How could Lexie Court, *the* Lexie Court, just disappear? "Did her mother go, too?"

"I doubt it."

So Mrs. Court finally got rid of her, just discarded her own daughter like garbage. After everything Lexie put me through, I should be glad her mother threw her out. And yet all I feel is empty, and a little sad.

Beth Ann doesn't seem to feel anything. Doesn't she even care that her best friend is gone, maybe for good? She samples another eye shadow. "Mrs. Court couldn't stand Lexie. Hated her. Lexie thought I didn't know, but I picked up on it a long time ago. Her mother's a total alkie, too, by the way. And I'm pretty sure she's a lezzie. She's definitely bi. Imagine if that ever got out. Whoa."

Whoa is right. I'm stunned. Speechless. Beth Ann knew everything, all this time. Her coldness is even more shocking. It's like she has no soul.

My face must give me away, because Beth Ann bursts out laughing. "What, did Lexie swear you to secrecy? Price-less. I bet you think you're the only one who knows about her mother's 'friend,' too. God, Peyton, you're the only one who sweats a secret. Secrets aren't for keeping. They're like cash—for spending. But then, you wouldn't know about that either."

I step back from the counter, weak-kneed. I thought secrets were about trust. My own secrets were never really secret. Everyone knew about my crush on Von, about my financial situation. And what I thought was my deepest, darkest secret was probably the most transparent: that I would have—and did—sell myself and my best friend out to be an Alpha, to be in Lexie's pocket.

Maybe nobody's secrets are secret. Like how everybody knew about Maya's mom's breast implants. Truth happens, whether you want it to or not. Somebody always knows. Somebody always tells.

Beth Ann is still watching me. "You don't really think you ever replaced me, do you?"

"What?"

"Thought you were her new BFF? That I was out of the picture because I was with Justin so much?"

"No, I never thought that." *I did. I fantasized about it.*

"You know, you're sweet, but you're not the sharpest tool in the shed."

"Excuse me?"

"You were the back-up plan, the fall guy in case anything went wrong."

"The fall guy?"

"It was my suggestion to use you, but Lexie never gave me credit for anything. She treated me like shit. Truth is, she needed me. She always used my ideas and pretended they were hers."

"What do you mean, your 'suggestion to use' me?"

"Peyton, Peyton, Peyton. You were the perfect choice, especially with your locker next to Smellika's. When Lexie snapped her fingers, you came running. Why do you think she all-of-a-sudden gave you rides everywhere and moved you into her locker?" Her words are like sharp hooks, digging and twisting my insides, gouging, biting, stinging. I shake my head, not wanting to believe. "The closer you were to Lexie, the more she could get you to do. And if anything went wrong, she could just slap it all on you."

Her lips curl into a sick grin. "We played you like a board game."

I step back, away from the counter, away from her. "Why? Why me? Why not Devin? She did way more to Ellika than me."

"Like we would have screwed Devin. My mom and her mom are on the same tennis team. Lexie's been on cruises with her family. We've hung out with her forever. No, like I said, you were the perfect choice. You were on the squad but you weren't really one of us. And you were so easy. 'You're the strongest base on the squad.' Isn't that what she told you?" The memory of Lexie's compliment comes flooding back. How easily I'd been fooled, how blind I'd been. How stupid.

The day they sweet-talked me into stealing Ellika's uniform, that's when it started. *Look at those long legs, Peyton … I'm so jealous … you're so lucky …* I was flattered by the attention, even more flattered that out of the whole squad, they'd picked me. *Why does it have to be stealing?* I'd thought. *Why couldn't they have chosen me for something else?*

I was chosen for something else. Handpicked. Stealing the uniform was only the beginning. They'd planned to use me as a scapegoat for Operation Smellika from Day One. They buttered me up to fry me.

It's all how you spin it, Lexie said. I was the spin. Me.

I want to punch her. Hard. I want to put my hands around her throat and squeeze. I want to wipe the arrogant grin off her face. She's enjoying this. "You ate it up, too. 'Ooh, Peyton, you're the only one I trust.' I know all the phony crap she told you. You worshiped her." Her eyes are twinkling. "Don't you get it, base? You were the best one for her to walk all over. You were smiling while she was fucking standing on you."

A wave of fury crashes into me and pours out. I lean over the counter and get right in her face. I'm not so vulnerable anymore, not so easily manipulated. "If you bitches thought this was all some board game, then who won?"

"What?"

"Who won? I'm still at Beachwood, and so is Ellika. And where are you? At some crappy B-list school where nobody knows you. So it looks like your little game didn't work. Lexie couldn't slap it all on me. And now she's gone. And so are you. So I guess you're not the sharpest tool in the shed, either, Beth Ann. Because you're the one that got slapped."

"For now." She shrugs. "Maybe. But you and I both know I'll still be popular wherever I go. So will Lexie. We'll always run with the right people, be in the spotlight. In high school, in college, even after. You, on the other hand, won't. That's just how it is." She turns and starts to walk away.

I know what she says is probably true. The Beth Anns

and Lexies are the beautiful people. They have wealth and charm and status. They're born into it, and they stay in it. I'll probably live a very different life than the lives they'll have.

Thank God.

Because I have to believe there is payback on some level. "Beth Ann!" She whirls around, all attitude, her Scarlett Johansson lips pursed, no doubt wondering what I could possibly have to say after the bombs she's been dropping. What I should be saying is thank you, because if I've learned anything from her and the squad, it's how to talk like a bitch. *Sometimes you have to be a bitch to get what you want . . .*

And what I want is to slice her to pieces. "Maybe you're right. Maybe you will end up in the spotlight at Palm Glades Prep, but you'll never really be the big star there, will you? I mean, they must already have some Lexie-type running the show. You'll probably end up like you are now, in the popular crowd but with no *real* friends, except for a so-called best friend who tells you you're fat and stupid all the time."

The smug grin is gone.

"Because the truth is, Beth Ann, you're no Lexie. At least people either love or hate Lexie, or both, but nobody cares one way or the other about you. You've always been a sidekick, a hanger-on. An afterthought." Her hand, resting on the strap of her bag, is trembling. It gives me strength. "And maybe after high school and college, you'll still 'run with the right people,' but maybe you'll end up like Lexie's mother, a drunk with a kid she hates and a husband who left her alone to rot. Maybe you'll live a useless life that doesn't matter to anybody."

She's looking right into my eyes. I'm getting to her. This is better than squeezing her neck.

"Maybe you'll always be popular, but one day you'll disappear, to Switzerland, maybe, and no one will care."

The saleswoman appears behind her. "Ready for me to ring you up now, hon?"

I answer before Beth Ann can open her mouth. "Yeah, she's ready. We're done."

31

Ryan's house is only a short bus ride from my apartment. I tell the guard at the gate that he's expecting me, even though he isn't. But I'm sure he's home. Where else would he be at ten on a Saturday morning? He's probably just watching TV or something.

Even if he isn't home, I still want to drop off his trig guide in person. It's made of copies from all these different textbooks and websites he found. He left it at my apartment. Every day during my suspension, Ryan came over after school and tutored me. And yesterday was the greatest math moment of my life: I got an eighty-five on my trig quiz. Me, an eighty-five! I have a lot to thank him for, and not just my trig grades. So I figure the least I can do is thank him in person.

I ring the doorbell. A man with Ryan's face and gray hair answers. "Hello," he says.

"Uh, hi. I'm Peyton Grady. I'm a friend of Ryan's."

A mix of surprise and delight passes over his face. "Well, come on in, Peyton. I'm Ryan's dad." He shakes my hand. "Ryan's on the patio, out by the pool. I'd walk you there, but I have to get back to a conference call, so just go straight until you get to the French doors. You won't miss it."

This is a big house. I spot a photo of Ryan's dad in a NASA uniform, holding a space helmet. He looks a lot younger. Beyond the French doors, there's a humongous pool. Ryan is sitting at a glass table under an umbrella. It looks like he's tinkering with little pieces of electronic machinery. He's so engrossed in what he's doing, he doesn't even notice me. There are tools all over the table with small metal pieces and wires everywhere.

And two scuba diving suits lying across the chair next to him.

I open the doors. Ryan doesn't look up. "Hey, dad. I think I fixed this one. Both robots should work now, when I put everything back together." I walk past him to the edge of the pool and look down. There they are. Two pool tables, just like he said.

"Peyton!" He gets up. I stare at him, open-mouthed. He has the same expression. "What are you doing here?"

I hand him his trig guide. "You have pool tables down there."

"Is that why you came over? To see for yourself?"

"No, I—"

"You thought I was lying. Like everyone else." He's hurt.

"No, no, of course not," I say, trying to hide the complete astonishment in my voice. "I never thought that."

I wish I could tell him that although I did buy into the common belief that he's a liar, now I know better. I've learned the hard way that things aren't always what they seem to be, and you can't ever just believe the hype. You have to find out for yourself how people really are.

Maybe I'll be able to tell him all that some day, but right now all I can manage is, "I actually came here to return your trig guide." It's hard to get the words out. "And to say thank you. You helped me with so much. And not just with tutoring. You were really there for me when the going got tough."

He shrugs, with a flash of dimples. "I was happy to be there."

I wish I could do something to show him my gratitude. Maybe I should have brought a gift. And then I realize I do have something I can give him. "It's *Chiquitita*," I say.

"What?"

"My middle name. It's *Chiquitita*."

"Your name is Peyton *Chiquitita* Grady?"

"'Fraid so. It was the name of my parents' favorite ABBA song."

"That's the most original middle name I've ever heard."

"Thanks. You're the most original person I know."

"Thanks." Awkward pause. Then, "I thought it was supposed to be a secret. The name, I mean."

"I don't have that many secrets anymore."

"Oh. Um, want to play a game of pool? We have an extra scuba suit."

"Oh, I can't. I'm meeting Maya and Jamar at the dollar theater."

"Oh."

"But I'd love to, some other time." As I'm saying it, I realize I'm not just being polite. I really would like to try it. It's got to be fun. "Seriously. Another time."

"Sure. What are you seeing?"

"One of the *Star Wars* movies. I'm not sure which one. They're having a *Star Wars* marathon."

"I love those movies." This revelation is not exactly a shocker. I'm sure he would have said the same thing if it was a *Lord of the Rings* marathon. His invisible tail is wagging. It's that puppy-dog quality. I have to say it. I don't have the will to resist. "Want to come?"

He lights up like a Jedi's lightsaber. "Sure. Let me get my keys."

There was a time I wouldn't have been caught dead with Ryan/Compular Blum at the movies. But that was before I knew what a true friend really was. Things have changed. I've changed. The fog has lifted and I can see people more clearly now, including myself. Maybe I'll always envy the "in" crowd a little. But I know what's important now. I was lucky to have Ryan around when my life was falling apart, and I like having him around now. There's no new Peyton or old Peyton anymore. There's just me.

And I am very okay with just me.

The End

©Barbara Taylor

About the Author

Debbie Reed Fischer was a cheerleader briefly at a private high school in Europe (not Switzerland). She loved writing all the cheers, but admits, "We may have been the worst cheerleaders on the planet. None of us could even do the splits." Fortunately, when she wasn't cheering badly, she had a lot of time to read. Visit her at DebbieReedFischer.com.